About Mike

M.W. Craven was born in Carlisle and grew up in Newcastle. He joined the army at sixteen, and left ten years later to gain a degree in social w[illegible]. He worked for seventeen [illegible] officer in Cumbria before [illegible] author. *The Puppet S*[illegible] book in his Washington Poe series, was published in 2018 and won the Crime Writers' Association Gold Dagger. The fourth in the series, *Dead Ground*, was published in June 2021 and became a *Sunday Times* bestseller.

Keep in touch with Mike.

@MWCravenUK

m.w.craven

MikeCravenAuthor

https://www.mwcraven.com

Also by M.W. Craven

Washington Poe series

The Puppet Show

Black Summer

The Curator

Dead Ground

The Botanist

Cut Short (short story collection)

Avison Fluke series

Born in a Burial Gown

Body Breaker

THE CUTTING SEASON

M.W. CRAVEN

CONSTABLE

CONSTABLE

First published in Great Britain in 2022 by Constable

3 5 7 9 10 8 6 4

A CIP catalogue record for this book is available from the British Library.

ISBN: 978-1-47213-519-3

Typeset in Stone Serif by SX Composing DTP, Rayleigh, Essex
Printed and bound in Great Britain by Clays Ltd, Elcograf S.p.A.

Papers used by Constable are from well-managed forests and other responsible sources.

Constable
An imprint of
Little, Brown Book Group
Carmelite House
50 Victoria Embankment
London EC4Y 0DZ

An Hachette UK Company
www.hachette.co.uk

www.littlebrown.co.uk

A little bit about Washington Poe

It started with an old lady.

An old lady who had stepped in front of a train.

There were gangsters and bent cops and a contract killer called the Pale Man, but they were not as important as the old lady. And neither was the dead good man who turned out to be a dead *bad* man.

In the years that followed, some people would forget about the old lady. They would forget that, if it was not for her, none of this would have happened. Nobody would have been murdered. Nobody would have dangled from a meat hook in a cold warehouse. Nobody would have called in the Pale Man.

Washington Poe would never forget about the old lady, though.

Poe was a detective sergeant in the National Crime Agency. He had been involved in many weird cases, but he would remember this case for as long as he lived. His part in the story did not start with the old lady. It started when he was told to go to Bristol. He went there to see if someone really had eaten part of the dead good man, who would later turn out to be a dead bad man.

(Yes, *eaten*.)

Things had kind of got out of hand after that.

Later on, Washington Poe would dangle from a meat hook, his body bruised and battered. Then, the gangsters and the corrupt cop and the contract killer called the Pale Man all thought they had won. They thought they had won and Washington Poe had lost. They thought a man dangling from a meat hook was a stone-cold loser with no more cards left to play.

They were wrong.

Because Washington Poe knew two things they did not know.

The first thing was that he had a friend called Tilly Bradshaw. Tilly was possibly the cleverest person in the world. She knew a lot about maths and science and computers and things like that. She was not a police officer like Poe, but she did work with him. And in every case they worked, she always watched his back.

The second thing Poe knew was that he did not play by his rules, the police rules. He played by the criminals' rules. The gangsters and the corrupt cop and the contract killer known as the Pale Man did not know that.

But they would find out.

Oh yes they would.

Please, sir, one of my love handles is missing

The human body might look like a lump of meat held up by a skeleton and kept together with stretchy skin, but really it is a machine. It is a machine like a motorbike. The feet are the wheels and the bum is the seat. The mouth is the horn and the bones are the frame and handlebars. You do not want to know what the exhaust is.

The engine of this human motorbike is the heart. Without the heart there really is not much point in having a body. A body without a heart will not work – the same way a motorbike without an engine will not work. It does not matter how carefully you polish it or how much air you pump into the tyres. A motorbike without an engine is as much use as a waterproof teabag.

The heart sends fresh red blood to all the organs that need it, in the same way the engine sends fuel around the motorbike to make it work.

The heart sends blood around the body through a huge network of tubes. Some of the tubes are as thick as your thumb. Other tubes are too small to see. There are so many tubes that, if you laid them on the ground end to end, they would stretch around the Earth nearly three times.

Unfortunately for the man who was tied to the kitchen stool, a whole load of these tubes were not in his body any more. Along with some fat, some skin and some flesh, some of the tubes were lying in a bloody heap on the carpet. Two flies were playing about on the heap.

Detective Sergeant Washington Poe thought the man was missing about four hundred miles of tubes. That is roughly the distance between Glasgow and London. The heap looked like someone had dropped a bag of chopped liver on the carpet. The heap was not steaming now, but it would have been steaming when it was cut out of the man.

The man was naked and very, very dead. The rest of his body was pale and hairy but unharmed. Whoever had done this – because the man could not have done it to himself – had carved the flesh from the soft bit above one of the man's hips. Poe thought the soft bits were called love handles. They were soft and flabby and easy to slice through with a sharp blade.

The carpet beneath the stool and around the heap of flesh was dark red and crusty with blood. Poe thought the victim had probably passed out during the assault. He hoped he had anyway.

'First impressions?' a woman in a white crime scene suit asked Poe.

The woman was called Detective Chief Inspector Lucy Sampson. She was in charge. She was the cop who had called the National Crime Agency unit that Poe worked for. The unit investigated serial killers and weird murders. Poe could only see the eyes of DCI Lucy Sampson because she wore a face mask, but she looked worried.

Poe pointed towards the huge wound on the body of the dead man. 'It looks like someone was trying to take a pound of flesh,' he said.

'I suppose,' Sampson said. 'We thought that maybe someone wanted to eat his flesh.'

'Taking a pound of flesh has come to mean the punishment for an unpaid debt,' Poe said. 'I think someone felt that this man owed them something. When he would not give them what he owed them, they took his flesh. Nobody has eaten him, that is for sure.'

'That is a relief,' Sampson said. 'What happens next?'

'I think you need to meet Tilly Bradshaw.'

Would a salad kill you?

Three hours earlier.

In the National Crime Agency office, the last Friday afternoon of every month was 'Ask Tilly Anything Friday'. Poe had invented it in a hurry after his boss, Detective Inspector Stephanie Flynn, had asked him to come up with a team-building exercise everyone could do. She wanted something that would take their minds off the day job of hunting serial killers.

'Do something cheap and fun,' Flynn had said. Poe had said the pub was cheap and fun. She had told him to try harder. He promised he would, but then he forgot all about it.

Poe was like that.

So when Flynn asked what he had planned, he panicked. He said he had arranged for Tilly Bradshaw – the very awkward, very clever civilian in his team – to answer any question put to her. The stranger the question, the better.

He even told Flynn he had bought a hat for the questions to go in. (He had not bought a hat. He found one in a skip.) He would pick one question out of the hat at lunchtime. He would give Tilly one hour to prepare her answer.

'Are you taking the piss?' Flynn had asked. 'You have had a month and this is the best you can do?'

'It will be fun,' Poe said.

And it was.

Tilly had been hired by the unit to help work out who might be murderers by looking at lots of information. She seemed to know everything about everything. And if she was not sure about something, it did not take her long to become an expert. So the unit at the National Crime Agency knew they had a once-in-a-lifetime chance to get answers to anything that had been bothering them.

Most questions were along the lines of 'How many gas-filled balloons would I need to tie to my chair if I wanted to float like the old man from *Up*?', 'Do bug-eyed aliens exist?' and 'Could *Jurassic Park* really happen?' Some questions, like 'What would happen if all the bees died?', were more serious.

That afternoon's question was one of the silly ones. There had been three questions for

Poe to choose from. He told everyone he chose a question at random, but really he rooted through his hat until he found one he liked.

There were two questions – 'What happens if you only eat sausages?' and 'How much bacon is too bad for you?' – that were clearly from Tilly herself. The questions were part of Tilly's long-term attempt to change Poe's meat-based diet to a plant-based one. He had once told her he would rather set his teeth on fire than eat lentil soup.

So Poe had picked the third question – 'How big would the tidal wave be if everyone in the world went to the same place at the same time and jumped up and down?' He had given the question to Tilly at lunchtime and told her everyone would gather at two o'clock to hear her answer.

She had read the question and said, 'You didn't choose either of the other questions then, Poe?'

'You mean the ones from you?' Poe asked.

She folded her arms and scowled. 'Would a salad kill you?'

'I guess we will never know,' he replied. 'Anyway, I'm off out for a pie and a pint. Can I pick anything up for you?'

But Tilly had already opened her laptop.

How to eat a human

One hour later, Tilly had an answer to the question. It had not taken her long.

'Nothing,' she said.

'Nothing?' Poe asked. 'That is your answer? Nothing?'

She nodded.

'Are you sure?' Poe asked. 'If everyone in the world jumped up and down at the same time there would not be a giant tidal wave that completely covered America?'

'No,' Tilly said.

'What about an earthquake?' Poe asked.

'Again, no,' Tilly said.

'Not even a tiny one?' Poe said.

Tilly shook her head. 'The Earth is ten trillion times heavier than the combined weight of all humans, Poe,' she said. 'A pea landing on an elephant's back would have more impact.'

'How boring.'

'However,' Tilly said, 'the question misses the point. Everyone being in the same place at the same time would not cause a tidal wave, but it *would* have a terrible outcome.'

'It would?' asked Poe.

'Yes,' said Tilly. 'Between five and six billion people would die.'

'Perhaps we should not do it then,' Poe said.

'Why would so many people die, Tilly?' the office manager, a cheerful woman called Rhona, asked.

Tilly got to her feet and approached the whiteboard. She picked up a red pen and wrote 'Cumbria.'

'Let's imagine Cumbria is the place everyone turns up to,' she said. 'It could be anywhere of course, but Cumbria is where Poe is from and it is big enough for all the people in the world to stand in at the same time.'

'I hope they do not all want a cup of tea,' Poe said. 'I only have two mugs.'

'Pretend that the moment the last person arrives is the moment when we all jump up and down,' Tilly continued. 'Nothing will happen. About ten minutes later, some people will get bored and begin drifting away. And this is when the problem starts.'

'What problem?' Poe asked, interested despite himself.

'Cumbria, or anywhere else in the world for

that matter,' Tilly said, 'is not set up to cope with eight billion people, Poe. Even if all the boats and all the planes in the world turned up to help, it would take almost one thousand years to get everyone home again. And if there were eight billion people in Cumbria, the whole of the UK's food and fresh water would run out in just over a day. Almost all of the world's population would soon starve to death.'

'Blimey,' Poe said. 'And the only ones who would survive would be the ones who got away on the boats and planes in the first few days?'

'No, Poe,' Tilly said. 'That would barely be a fraction of the world's population. Most of the people who survived would be cannibals.'

'You mean the people on a meat-based diet would live,' he said, checking Flynn was still in her meeting in the conference room, 'and the people on a plant-based diet would die?'

Tilly scowled.

'Would you eat someone, Sergeant Poe?' Rhona asked.

Poe paused while he considered the question. 'Only if they were in a curry,' he said. 'Here, Tilly, pass me that marker pen . . .'

A tough sergeant

Which was why, ten minutes later, when Flynn walked out of the conference room, there was a drawing of a human body on the whiteboard. Poe had drawn different cuts of meat, like chops, steaks and shanks, on the body. It looked a bit like a butcher's picture of a cow.

'The trick would be to avoid well-exercised areas like the calf and thigh,' Poe said, pointing to the legs on his picture. 'Meat from this area will be tough and stringy. I would choose the upper arms or the shoulder, and I would cook the meat in the slow cooker. I would use some of the leg bones for stock. Maybe I would add some cider vinegar and root vegetables. A couple of Scotch bonnet chillies would liven up the taste a bit.'

Someone giggled.

'In fact, this is making me hungry,' he added. 'If anyone fancies going to that new barbeque place tonight, the ribs are on me.'

A big cheer went up.

Flynn stood and watched, a smile dancing across her lips. This was what she had wanted to happen when she had forced Poe into having the monthly team-building exercises. She had known he would bodge it, but she also knew it would not matter. The important thing was that the team enjoyed each other's company for a while without the pressure of work.

She also wanted the team to see a different side of Poe. All they usually saw was him being grumpy. They only saw the stubborn part of him that always wanted to do what was right, or what he thought was right. It made him a tough sergeant to work for. Watching him laughing and joking with his team was worth a wasted afternoon.

'How to eat a human?' Flynn said. 'Seriously, Poe, "Ask Tilly Anything Friday" is getting weirder and weirder.'

'Tilly wanted a decent recipe for a leg,' he replied. 'One with plenty of crackling.'

'I most certainly did not!' Tilly said. 'I am vegan.'

'Have you finished talking to Director Hanson?' Poe asked Flynn.

Flynn had been in a budget meeting all afternoon and Hanson had asked to speak to her afterwards. He wasn't the crime unit's director

– that was a man called Edward van Zyl – but Hanson hated Poe and never missed the chance to find out what he had been up to.

'I have,' Flynn replied.

'And?' asked Poe.

'The same as usual,' Flynn said. 'Hanson wanted to go through your expenses and overtime claims. He wanted to see if there was something he could tell you off for.'

'Fat chance,' Poe said. 'Tilly goes through my expenses before I submit them now.'

'Anyway,' Flynn said, pointing at the drawing of the butchered human. 'This is all strangely fitting.'

'It is?' Poe asked.

'Cops in Bristol think they have found the victim of a cannibal. Take Tilly and go and see what it is they *really* have.'

The late, great, David Gilchrist

'Did you know that England does not have a law against eating people, Poe?' Tilly said when Poe got back to the car after looking at the body of the dead man. 'In 1988 an artist called Rick Gibson legally ate some donated human tonsils in Walthamstow High Street in London. In 1989 he ate a slice of human testicle in Lewisham High Street.'

'He should go to Cumbria,' Poe grunted. 'See what happens when he tries that sort of thing up there.'

'Was it awful inside?' Tilly asked, pointing at the house.

'I have seen worse,' Poe replied. 'And it is not cannibalism.'

He talked her through what he had seen and his theory about an unpaid debt.

'Do we have a name for the victim?' Tilly asked.

'David Gilchrist. He was fifty-five years old. He ran the Maston Tree Foundation. They raise money and give it to small charities.'

'And you think he owed someone money?' Tilly said.

'It is somewhere to start,' Poe said.

A good man

It was somewhere to start, but not somewhere to finish.

Not according to Tilly.

'David Gilchrist had no debt, Poe,' she explained. 'None of his bank accounts were overdrawn and he had savings.'

'How did you find that out so quickly?' asked Poe.

'Hmm?' said Tilly.

'I said how did you find that out so quickly?'

Tilly did not even pretend to look guilty. Tilly treated firewalls and passwords and all the other kinds of online security in the same way Poe treated the fat and salt warnings on packets of sausages – they were to be ignored. The people who designed computer security had no idea someone as clever as Tilly even existed. They certainly had no chance of keeping her out.

'How much money did he have?' Poe asked.

'Thirty thousand pounds,' Tilly replied.

Not a huge amount of money for a man of his age, but more than Poe had.

'Was he stealing?' Poe asked.

'No, said Tilly. 'The Maston Tree Foundation is well run and it would be hard for someone to steal from it. I have checked their bank statements and there is no money missing.'

'Maybe he was getting bribes from the charities wanting grants?' Poe wondered.

Tilly shook her head. 'He had nothing to do with that part. A board of trustees, not Gilchrist, decided which charities got the money.'

'Was he on a big salary?' Poe asked.

'No,' Tilly replied. 'David Gilchrist's salary was set by the trustees and he agreed there would be a "charity discount" on the pay of all senior managers, including himself.'

'Charity discount?' asked Poe.

'It means that the staff working for the foundation do it because they want to help people, so they have to accept less pay than they would normally get.'

'OK,' Poe said. 'Gilchrist was not stealing, he was not getting bribes and he had no debt. So we can rule out money as the reason for his murder.'

'We can, Poe.'

'But someone *did* strap him to a chair and cut

a chunk of flesh out of him,' Poe said. 'Nobody does that without a reason.'

'Unless we are dealing with a serial killer,' Tilly pointed out.

Poe considered this. He would have heard if there had been any reports of a loony out there carving flesh out of people. Poe had caught many serial killers. He knew that their victims were either murdered quickly in their own homes, or taken somewhere quiet so the killer could take his time and enjoy it. But Gilchrist had died slowly due to blood loss in his own home.

'I do not think it is a serial killer, Tilly,' he said. 'I think someone had a reason for doing this, and not just because they enjoy murder. If we find out the reason, we will find out who did it.'

'I think you are right, Poe,' said Tilly. 'What shall we do now?'

'I'm sorry, Tilly, but I need you in that house.'

A Sergeant Poe voodoo doll

Detective Chief Inspector Lucy Sampson was not keen on letting a civilian into her crime scene. Poe tried to explain why she should allow Tilly into the house.

'If there is any electronic evidence, Tilly will find it,' he said. 'I do not care how well hidden it is. But she can only find it if she is allowed in the house.'

'She can examine Gilchrist's computer after it has been processed by the crime scene team, Sergeant Poe,' Sampson replied.

Poe shook his head. 'Tilly needs to see the computer before some dunce deletes something important. She will wear full forensic gear and she will leave everything as she finds it.'

'Not happening,' Sampson said.

'This is what our unit does,' Poe said. 'If you do not want our help, why did you call us?'

'I was ordered to,' Sampson said.

'You were ordered to?' said Poe. 'By who?'

'My chief constable,' Sampson replied.

'That is unusual,' Poe said. 'All the chief constables I know prefer keeping things in-house.'

'It is certainly the first time it has happened to me,' Sampson admitted.

'So I will need to speak to your chief about this,' Poe said. 'Do you have her number?'

With her bluff called, Sampson gave in. 'Fine,' she said. 'Tilly can go inside the house. But if this comes back on me, I am going to buy a Sergeant Poe voodoo doll and I will stick pins in it tonight.'

* * *

Tilly had never worn a forensic suit before. She crunched numbers and drew up information about suspects. Normally, there would be no need for her to attend a crime scene. This was not a normal crime, though.

For reasons unknown, a pound of flesh had been carved out of a good member of the public, and Poe did not think a stranger had done it. The murderer was more likely to be someone David Gilchrist had known, or someone who had known him. And that meant Poe wanted Tilly to search through Gilchrist's computer before Detective Chief Inspector Sampson sealed it up and took it away.

Sampson would argue that her force's crime unit was capable of checking the computer, but Poe did not think 'capable' would cut it this time. If the answer *was* on the victim's computer, it would not be obvious. It was likely to be found in the mess of stuff that people stored on their home computers – the photographs, the downloads, the bookmarks, the general tat.

Tilly would spot the email that did not seem quite right. She would notice the document that raised more questions than it answered, or the strange website Gilchrist had visited. In short, the computer needed to be looked at by someone who thought data was interesting. Someone who would not get bored.

In other words, someone like Tilly.

So Poe asked Tilly to suit up. She had to wear the disposable paper coveralls. The plastic overshoes with the elastic tops. The gloves, the face mask.

'Ready?' Poe asked.

Tilly gave him a double thumbs up.

'Do not touch anything until I say it is OK, Tilly.'

'OK, Poe.'

'Now,' Poe said, 'the detective chief inspector does not want us looking at David Gilchrist's laptop. If she argues again that her own computer experts must have a look first, leave the talking to me.'

'I will, Poe,' Tilly said.

'And if you can,' Poe continued, 'try to pretend you are . . .'

'Pretend I am what?' Tilly asked.

'You know, not . . . unusual,' Poe said.

'I will try my best, Poe.'

The Danish king

Tilly blew a raspberry through her face mask when Detective Chief Inspector Sampson suggested they wait for her computer guys.

'The police do not have computer experts, Detective Chief Inspector Lucy Sampson,' Tilly said. 'Anyone who knows anything about computers is working for private firms, and they are making lots of money.'

'You don't work for a private firm and you are an expert,' Poe said.

'Yes, but I am different,' Tilly replied.

'Tell me something I don't know,' Poe said.

'OK, Poe,' Tilly said. 'Bluetooth technology is named after the tenth-century Danish king, Harald Bluetooth.'

'No,' said Poe, 'I didn't mean . . . what, really?'

'Yes, Poe. King Harald Bluetooth united the tribes and formed the Kingdom of Denmark,' Tilly explained. 'The company who invented Bluetooth are Scandinavian and they thought it would be neat to name something that unites devices after the king who united their kingdoms.'

'And why was this king called Bluetooth?' Poe asked.

'I'm a scientist, not a dumb-as-a-doorknob dentist, Poe,' she replied. 'How would I know?'

Sampson stared in surprise. Poe didn't bat an eyelid. On the Tilly weirdness scale, this barely registered.

'Is she . . . er, OK?' Sampson whispered to Poe.

'Tilly has an unusual way of working,' Poe replied, 'but she is the best there is.'

'She is the best in the National Crime Agency?' Samson asked.

'In the world,' Poe replied.

'Gosh.'

'And despite outward appearances,' Poe said, 'I can assure you she's perfectly normal. Although for some reason she thinks dentists are stupid.'

'Go for it then,' Sampson said. 'If anyone asks, I'll say I asked for help in drawing up an early list of family, friends and acquaintances. I assume you think as I do? That whoever did this murder knew the victim?'

Poe nodded.

Tilly cleared her throat. 'Without specific intelligence, drawing up a list of friends and so on is pointless, Detective Chief Inspector Lucy Sampson,' she said.

'It's standard police work, Tilly,' Sampson replied. 'It might not be glamorous enough for the National Crime Agency, but it is what we do here. We draw up lists of people and then we check those lists.'

Sampson may as well have said nothing.

Tilly continued, 'By the time someone gets to Mr Gilchrist's age, a person will on average have one hundred and fifty friends and colleagues. If you add family members and people from their childhood that figure rises to around four hundred.'

'OK, that *is* too many,' said Sampson.

'Please don't interrupt, Detective Chief Inspector Lucy Sampson,' Tilly said. 'I'm only halfway through what I was saying.'

Under his mask, Poe smiled.

Sampson held up her hands. 'Sorry,' she said.

Tilly carried on. 'And if the person we are looking for is actually a friend of a friend, then the number of people rises to one hundred and sixty-three thousand.'

Sampson looked stunned. 'How do you know this?'

'I did the maths in my head while you were talking to Poe,' Tilly said.

Sampson looked at Poe and raised her eyebrows.

'When I said she was normal I may have lied slightly,' Poe admitted.

Four seconds

'This won't take long, Detective Chief Inspector Lucy Sampson,' Tilly said. 'I will transfer everything on to my computer, then examine it in Poe's car.'

'Don't you need David Gilchrist's password?' Sampson asked.

After Poe and Tilly had stopped laughing, Poe said, 'Tilly doesn't believe in other people's passwords.'

'How long will it take her to crack . . .'

'I have finished,' Tilly said.

'About four seconds then,' Sampson said.

David Gilchrist's laptop had probably been shiny and new when he bought it, but even to Poe, who knew nothing about computers, it now looked bulky and clunky and terribly dated. Modern laptops, like the one Tilly had just taken from her bag, were sleek and light and as thin as a pencil.

Tilly linked her laptop to Gilchrist's computer with a cable she took from her pocket. Poe watched her quickly type out some code and, in under a minute, everything on Gilchrist's computer was on her laptop.

Tilly closed the lid and said, 'You can take this away now, Detective Chief Inspector Sampson. Please may I have David Gilchrist's phone and iPad?' She held out her hand.

Wordlessly, Sampson passed them over. 'OK, I believe you,' Sampson said to Poe. 'Can she do anything else?'

'She is the best person at her job that I have ever met,' Poe said. 'She spots patterns when no one else can and she develops computer programs that solve even the most difficult problems.'

'She sounds amazing,' Sampson said.

'She is,' Poe replied. 'She's probably the most important person in the National Crime Agency. So far, she has helped us catch eight serial killers and two serial rapists and solve many murders. She's also the most loyal friend I have ever had.'

'Is there anything she *cannot* do?' Sampson asked.

Poe looked at his friend. Tilly's fingers were typing so fast they blurred. Her eyes stared through her thick, round glasses at her laptop screen. She paused to tuck a stray hair behind her ear.

He smiled. 'She doesn't know when someone is being sarcastic,' he said.

Not such a good man then

'David Gilchrist was not a very nice man,' Poe said.

'What?' Sampson replied. 'Of course he was a nice man. You said it yourself. He started his foundation from scratch and over the years they have donated millions of pounds to good causes. He takes a tiny salary and he has not been stealing or taking bribes.'

'And that's true,' Poe confirmed. 'Nothing Tilly has found suggests otherwise. Everything was above board and his foundation was a leader in its field.'

'What is the problem then?' Sampson asked. 'He's a hero in Bristol. They will probably put up a statue of him.'

'Yeah, but they will have to tear it down afterwards,' Poe said.

'I'm not sure I follow,' Sampson said.

'The problem is the way he went about his

fundraising,' Poe said. 'He was basically running a boiler room.'

'Boiler room?'

'Cold callers using high-pressure sales tactics. Mr Gilchrist would buy lists of the names of so-called "generous people" from other charities – sucker lists he called them – and his team would ruthlessly target them.'

'Good grief,' Sampson said.

'Tilly found the script his staff worked from,' Poe said. 'It was on his laptop, hidden in a secret folder. They were told not to accept no for an answer and to hit potential and current donors like a sledge-hammer. Those are Gilchrist's words, not mine. His team's standard line was "there is no excuse not to donate", but there were several other lines like that. They would say anything to squeeze cash out of the person on the other end of the phone.'

Sampson glanced at the dead man again, this time with less sympathy.

'There was also the constant drip-feed of begging letters landing on people's doormats,' Poe continued. 'Some were getting forty or fifty letters a week. Tilly says they all used carefully chosen language. The words and pictures were designed to make people feel sympathy and guilt. There were photographs of abused dogs, starving children, caged bears – the type of thing you see on daytime TV.'

'How horrid,' said Sampson.

'And Gilchrist didn't stop there,' Poe continued. 'Tilly discovered he also bought lists of names of known donors from dodgy firms. Hundreds of thousands of names. He wanted to find old people suffering from confusion, memory problems and terminal illnesses. He paid a lot of money for those lists.

'His staff would call these poor people, pressure them into signing up to direct debits for one of his animal abuse charities, then call back the next day and sign them up to a charity donating to cancer research. Tilly has found people on his computer who have direct debits to over twenty of Gilchrist's charities. Some of them are in their nineties and have dementia. One of them got into so much debt she had to sell her house.'

'Oh dear, that's awful,' Sampson said. 'There's something I don't understand, though. If Gilchrist was the horrible man you claim he was, what was in it for him? We know he didn't benefit from this in terms of money.'

'You said it yourself,' Poe said. 'He was the local hero. They will erect a statue. *That* was what was in it for him. The glory, the status.

The social standing it gave him. The invites to the parties, the headlines in the newspapers. His OBE for services to charity.'

'Does any of this help, though?' Sampson asked. 'You said he bought lists of hundreds of thousands of names. That is far too big a suspect pool for my team to go through.'

'Ah, but your team does not have a Tilly,' Poe said.

'She will help?' Sampson asked. 'She'll go through the names?'

'She's already run her program,' Poe said.

'And?'

Poe opened the laptop he was holding. Carefully. This was Tilly's laptop and was probably worth thousands of pounds. He pointed at the screen. It showed part of a list. One of the names had been highlighted. 'Do you recognise this name?' he asked.

Sampson leaned forward and read the name. Understanding flashed across her face.

'Oh no,' she said.

Dorothy Pewter

Dorothy Pewter had been on the national news two months earlier, and not in a good way. She was the old lady who had stood on platform four at Bristol Temple Meads station and stepped in front of the 12:04 train to London Paddington. The neat and tidy eighty-four-year-old was turned into something that looked like a burst bag of mince. She didn't leave a note and there was no clear reason for her to kill herself.

'We looked into her death,' Sampson said. 'Despite the lack of a suicide note, it was definitely a suicide. We checked the station's CCTV cameras and there was no one standing near her when she stepped off the platform. We thought it was because she was being treated for stomach cancer. Do you think she's connected to David Gilchrist?'

Poe nodded. 'Gilchrist ranked his donors,' he said, 'and Dorothy Pewter was near the top of the list. She was one of the people his sales team called every day. Tilly says there were days when she received up to forty phone calls, all of them begging for money, all from Gilchrist's team. If she had already set up a direct debit for a charity, his sales team were told to ask for a one-off donation. When she did that, they would call back and ask her to increase her direct debit payment.

'When she received her cancer diagnosis Gilchrist somehow found out and his sales team began hounding her to change her will. They wanted her to leave some money to a charity, and when she did, they wanted her to leave money to another one as well. They told her it was her duty.'

'Bastards!' Sampson snapped. 'Absolute bastards!'

Poe said, 'Tilly says that when Dorothy died, over a thousand pounds a month was going to various Gilchrist charities, and she had changed her will so he would get her house too.'

'He drove her to suicide then,' Sampson said.

'He did,' Poe agreed.

'Why didn't we find any evidence of this?' Sampson asked. 'We had a team check her house for a suicide note and they would have noticed if her hallway was full of begging letters.'

'That's the question, isn't it?' Poe said. 'Why *didn't* you notice something was amiss?'

'I sent one of my best detectives,' Sampson replied.

'I'm sure you did,' Poe said. 'But I think the reason you didn't notice anything was because someone had removed all evidence of wrongdoing on the charity's behalf. Mrs Pewter's direct debits were all cancelled. The changes to her will were cancelled. Her bank accounts were refilled with money. Whoever did this was also clever enough to go to her house and remove all the begging letters.'

'Gilchrist was covering his tracks?' Sampson asked.

'We don't think it was Gilchrist,' Poe said.

'Who then?' Sampson wondered. 'One of his sales team?'

'We don't think it was anyone involved in the charity,' Poe said. 'We think it was someone who wanted to deal with David Gilchrist himself. It was someone who knew that any link between Dorothy Pewter and David Gilchrist had to be cut if they were going to get away with his murder.'

'You said, "deal with David Gilchrist *himself*,"' Sampson pointed out. 'You have a suspect, don't you?'

'This is where it gets tricky,' Poe said. 'Tilly

drew up a list of Dorothy's family and one name in particular stood out.'

'Oh?'

'Michael Pewter, her son,' Poe said.

'I'll get a team to pick him up,' Sampson said. 'Apart from him being a cold-blooded killer, what else do we know about Michael Pewter?'

'Nothing,' Poe said.

'Nothing?' Sampson exclaimed. 'I thought you said Tilly was the best in the business?'

'She is,' Poe said. 'But she ran into a problem when she did her background check.'

'What problem?' asked Sampson.

Poe said, 'His name is flagged.'

Flagged

'Flagged? So he's probably an informant or a terrorist or something,' Sampson said. 'Who flagged him?'

'My lot,' Poe replied.

'The National Crime Agency?' Sampson asked.

'Yep.'

'Why?' Sampson asked. 'Is he one of your snitches?'

'I don't know yet,' Poe said. 'Tilly refused to breach the security on his file. She's weird like that. She had been examining Dorothy Pewter's bank accounts all afternoon, but she would not check why her own agency is all over Michael.'

'Why?' Sampson said.

'She said they would know it was me,' Poe explained, 'and she doesn't like to see my boss yell at me.'

'I'll get my chief constable to put in a request,' Sampson said. 'We can claim special circumstances. Surely a murder investigation has a higher priority than whatever it is you guys have going on.'

Poe shrugged. The National Crime Agency had many units. None of them talked to each other, and they all thought whatever they were doing was more important than whatever anyone else was doing. This was annoying to Poe, who *knew* whatever he was doing was by far the most important thing happening in the agency.

'You don't think my chief will get permission?' Sampson asked.

'I don't think she will need to ask,' Poe replied.

'Why not?' said Sampson.

'Because,' Poe said, 'I think we are just about to be told.'

Poe nodded towards the street. A black Range Rover had just pulled up. Two serious-looking men got out. One was tall, one wasn't. They wore identical suits and, almost as if they had practised beforehand, they put on their sunglasses at exactly the same time.

'I think the cavalry's arrived,' Poe said. He paused a beat then added, 'What a pair of dickheads.'

Dumb and Dumber

Poe named the tall chap Dumb and the smaller chap Dumber. Dumb tried to swagger through the police barrier – the outer cordon – that had been put up outside the house. He was holding his ID badge in the air like it was the Olympic Torch. The uniformed constable by the barrier stopped Dumb in his tracks. Poe, just inside Gilchrist's house, listened at the door. He very much enjoyed the exchange.

'You can't come in unless my chief inspector gives you permission, sir,' the constable said.

'Go and get him then,' Dumb said.

'She's a she, sir,' the constable said.

'Go and get *her* then,' Dumb said.

'She's inside the house.'

'And?'

'I'm the outer cordon officer, sir,' the constable patiently explained.

'So what?' Dumb said.

'I can't leave my post until my chief inspector says I can,' the constable said.

'Shout for her then.'

'You have obviously never met my chief inspector, sir,' the constable chuckled. 'She would wear my nuts for earrings if I shouted for her.'

Poe sniggered. Cops were brilliant at following rules in order to annoy jumped-up dickheads. They always had been. By now Dumber had joined Dumb. Dumber remained silent.

'What do you expect me to do then?' Dumb asked the constable. 'I need to speak to her.'

'Do you have her number, sir?' the constable said politely. 'I'm sure she has her mobile on her.'

'No, I don't have her bloody number!' Dumb shouted.

'Ah, that's a shame, sir.'

'Do you have it?'

'Unfortunately not, sir,' said the constable. 'But I can ask her for it.'

'Do that then,' said Dumb. 'And be quick about it!'

'I'll have to wait until she comes outside first, sir,' the constable said. 'I can't leave my post, you see?'

'Oh for God's sake!'

Poe laughed loudly.

Dumb looked to the doorway Poe was leaning against. 'Who's that?' Dumb said to Dumber.

Dumber whispered something in his ear.

'Sergeant Poe?' Dumb said. '*Our* Sergeant Poe? That prick from the serial killer unit? I might have known he would be behind all this.'

'I can hear you, you know,' Poe said, grinning.

'Sergeant Poe, may we have a word?' Dumb said.

A person of interest

Dumber's name was Donald and Dumb's was Barry. They were both sergeants in the organised crime unit. They were not happy about being dragged away from their fancy office in London.

'Why have you been looking at Michael Pewter, Sergeant Poe?' Donald, the short one, asked.

Poe was sitting in the driver's seat of his car. Detective Chief Inspector Sampson was in the passenger seat. Barry and Donald were in the back. Tilly had gone to buy a bottle of water.

'This is a murder investigation,' Poe said. 'Why do you think we are looking at him?'

'He's a suspect?' Donald asked.

'A person of interest,' Poe said.

'Who's the victim?' Donald said.

Poe explained what had happened to David Gilchrist. He didn't tell Donald and Barry what had led him and Tilly to Michael Pewter. In his experience, the organised crime boys were all take, no give.

'Michael Pewter has no connections in Bristol,' Barry, the tall one, said.

'That's odd. His mum lived here,' Poe said.

'I mean, he has no *business* connections in Bristol,' Barry said.

'And what business would that be?' Sampson asked.

'I can't say,' Barry said. 'And while I have every sympathy, you can't speak to him.'

'Why not?' Poe asked.

'Let's just say he is off limits,' Barry said. He seemed to be the senior sergeant.

'Let's *not* say that,' Poe replied. 'Instead, why don't we say this is a murder investigation and Detective Chief Inspector Sampson here has a valid line of enquiry?'

'Tough,' said Barry. 'I'm telling you, you can't.'

'You can't tell me anything, mate,' Poe responded. 'I do not work for you, you do not outrank me and this is a murder investigation. As far as I'm concerned, that trumps whatever *Godfather* rubbish you have going on.'

'And the National Crime Agency certainly does not outrank Avon and Somerset Police,' Sampson snapped at Barry. 'So, either tell us what you know about Michael Pewter or get the hell away from my crime scene.'

'I'm sorry,' Barry said, 'but if necessary I will get our director-general to tell your chief constable to stop this investigation. That *is* a power we have.'

Sampson frowned. Barry was right. The boss of the National Crime Agency *did* have the power to tell chief constables what to do. Poe decided to help Sampson out. Sampson was a good cop and the organised crime sergeants were idiots.

'Here is what's going to happen if you don't tell us what we want to know,' Poe said to Barry and Donald. 'As soon as you have gone I'm going to get my colleague to plaster Michael Pewter's face all over social media. She will make him the most famous murder suspect in the country.'

'You're bluffing,' Barry said.

'You don't know me at all, do you?' Poe said.

'We'll have your colleague's badge,' Barry growled. 'You may not care about your career, Sergeant Poe, but I doubt you will throw someone else under the bus.'

Donald leaned in and whispered urgently in Barry's ear. Barry scowled, then frowned, then looked worried.

'This colleague wouldn't be Tilly Bradshaw, would it?' Barry asked Poe.

'I couldn't possibly say,' Poe said, 'but if it is her, you know you will never prove where anything came from. In fact, if you look, you might even find it came from one of your own social media accounts.'

The fact neither of them argued meant Tilly's skill and her loyalty to Poe were well known, even to the dumb knuckle draggers in the organised crime unit.

'Look,' Poe said, giving a bit of ground. 'Tell us what we need to know and, if Detective Chief Inspector Sampson agrees, it will go no further than this car. She can then make a decision about what she wants to do next, but anything she does do will go through formal channels.'

Donald and Barry didn't respond.

'Come on, guys, this is the best offer you are going to get all day,' Poe continued. 'And if you know of Tilly, you'll know she can look behind any firewall you have set up anyway. At least this way you get to appear helpful.'

Nothing.

'I'll start you off, shall I?' Poe sighed. 'Two National Crime Agency sergeants don't race across from London because one of their informants is in a bit of trouble, not unless he's involved in something big. How am I doing?'

Still nothing.

'OK, then,' Poe continued. 'But I have a problem with this theory. If Michael Pewter's snitching for you, having him on the hook for murder is a good thing, not a bad thing. Having a murder charge dangling over his head could prove useful when it comes to making sure he helps you. If he doesn't do what you want him to do, he goes to prison for twenty years.'

Barry and Donald glanced at each other.

'Michael Pewter isn't a paid informant at all, is he?' Poe said.

Donald looked at Barry. Barry nodded permission.

'No, Sergeant Poe, he's not an informant,' Donald said.

'What is he then?' Poe asked.

'He's a hired killer.'

The Pale Man

'Michael Pewter works for the Hole in the Wall Gang,' Barry said. 'They are a crew working out of Croydon in south London.'

'Why is that name familiar?' Poe asked.

'They have styled themselves after the famous Las Vegas burglary gang from the seventies and early eighties,' Barry explained. 'The Las Vegas gang were famous for drilling through walls and ceilings to get to the locations they burgled.'

'I remember,' Poe said. He had been to Vegas when he was in the army and had studied its crime history on the flight over. It was the FBI that had nicknamed them the Hole in the Wall Gang.

Poe, Tilly and the detectives had moved from the crime scene to a Bristol pub. Poe, offering an olive branch, said he would buy Barry and Donald a drink. Tilly was having sparkling water, no ice, and Sampson was having a Coke. Poe and the organised crime sergeants all had pints of Low Rider, a local pale ale.

Barry took a long drink, wiped off his foam moustache and continued. 'Anyway, the Croydon Hole in the Wall Gang is old-school,' he said. 'They don't sell drugs or women and they don't do extortion. The gang is run by a man called Frank Mason. He goes by the nickname Fatty Scraps.'

'Fatty Scraps?' Poe said. 'You're kidding, right?'

'If you saw him, you wouldn't say that,' Barry said. 'He's a big man. He runs his crew with an iron fist.'

'Fair enough,' said Poe. 'But if they don't do the usual gangster stuff, what *do* they do?'

'They do armed robberies mainly,' Barry explained. 'They raid banks, security vans, jewellers' shops, precious metal warehouses. Sometimes they burgle rich people's houses. That type of thing. They don't do many jobs but what they do is done well. And they are careful with what they take. So far they haven't been caught with so much as a stolen diamond.'

'There must be slim pickings in Croydon,' Poe said. 'I assume they travel for jobs?'

'All over Europe,' Barry confirmed. 'But they own a few pubs, restaurants and betting shops to launder the money they get from their fences. All of these are in Croydon. They are places they can protect. They pay dues to the bigger crews, but otherwise they keep what they earn.'

'What do they need a hit man for then?' Poe said.

'Michael is a legacy of the old days,' Barry said. 'After the East End had an influx of migrants in the seventies and eighties, a lot of cockney gangs moved to south London. The gangs there had to be persuaded to make room, and it rarely came down to a chat over tea and cakes. Finding a new manor became a cut-throat business. Michael Pewter was one of the most feared enforcers in south London.'

'And now?' Poe asked.

'Like I said, the Hole in the Wall Gang are old school. Fatty Scraps isn't going to abandon Michael Pewter just because he belongs in another era. And all the other gangs *know* he's there. Having Michael in your crew means people will think twice about messing with you.'

'Tell me about Pewter,' Poe asked.

Barry shrugged. 'Not much is known, to be honest,' he said. 'He's sixty-two. He has that condition where patches of his skin lose their colour. I forget what it's called. It mainly affects his face and hands and neck. Over the years he's become as white as an albino. His name on the street is the Pale Man. He's known for using a cut-throat razor, which fits with what you claim happened to your victim. Mess with the Pale Man and you get a wet neck.'

'He sounds like a Bond villain,' Poe said.

'A Bond *henchman* maybe,' Barry replied. 'As fearsome as he is, he has a weird code of honour. He expects people to keep their word, and he only takes jobs against his own kind. Criminals. No civilians.'

'He hacked a lump of flesh out of our victim,' Poe said. 'Pewter probably watched Gilchrist bleed to death.'

'That's what happens when you mess with the wrong person's mum, I suppose,' Barry said.

Poe drained his pint and nodded. He had some thinking to do.

Sparklers can give a nasty burn

After Barry and Donald had left, Poe said, 'David Gilchrist was responsible for the death of a professional killer's mother? That's just bad luck.'

Sampson nodded. 'I wonder what the odds are,' she said.

'It's the same as being killed by a firework,' Tilly said without missing a beat.

'How can you possibly know that?' Poe said.

'Duh, it's basic maths,' Tilly replied.

'It is?'

Tilly sighed. It was a noise Poe had grown used to. It was back-to-school time.

'There are about twelve million old people in the UK, of which fifty-five per cent are female,' Tilly explained. 'Our own records tell us there are fewer than twenty active hired killers at any one time. That means the chances of being responsible for the death of a hired killer's mother is around three hundred and thirty thousand to one.'

'And the fireworks bit?' Poe asked.

Tilly continued, 'The chance of being killed by a firework is three hundred and forty thousand to one, which is why I don't go outside on bonfire night.'

'Very sensible, Tilly,' Poe said. 'Sparklers can give you quite a nasty burn.'

Tilly nodded solemnly.

'What did they tell you when I was at the bar?' Sampson asked.

'I'm sorry?' Poe replied.

'I was watching you,' Sampson said. 'They leaned in and whispered something. You didn't look happy.'

'Oh, that? Usual rubbish,' Poe said. 'Stay away from their case, blah blah blah. I stopped listening after a while.'

'That's that then,' Sampson said. 'Nothing more we can do.'

'Why's that?' Poe asked.

'I can't go against an order from the National Crime Agency,' Sampson explained, 'and I don't imagine you will want to.'

Tilly laughed so hard that sparkling water came out of her nose. 'Poe doesn't care about things like that, Detective Chief Inspector Lucy Sampson!' she said, wiping tears from her eyes. 'In fact, telling him not to do something is usually the *worst* thing you can do. He's been to London to get told off by the director of our unit three times this year already.'

'Yes, thank you, Tilly,' Poe said.

'Once,' Tilly continued, 'he had to drive all the way to Aberdeen so he could apologise to the mayor, the skipper of a fishing trawler and an apprentice egg pickler.'

'I said, thank you, Tilly.'

'And last year he arrested a member of MI5,' Tilly added.

'I actually heard about that,' Sampson said, and grinned. 'What else has he done, Tilly?'

Poe put his head in his hands and groaned.

Ten minutes later, with Poe's history of ignoring orders well established, Sampson said, 'So what are we going to do now?'

Poe drained his pint. He put the glass back on the table with conviction. 'I don't know about you,' he said to Sampson, 'but I fancy a trip to Croydon.'

'Croydon?' Sampson repeated.

'I think it's about time I introduced myself to Fatty Scraps, don't you?' Poe looked at Tilly. 'We are going to need to do a few things first though, Tilly.'

Tilly nodded, all traces of fun and laughter gone.

It was time to go to work.

Battista's Bar and Grill

One week later.

Poe walked into Battista's Bar and Grill, one of the restaurants owned by Fatty Scraps, looking more confident than he felt. This was where the Hole in the Wall Gang hung out in Croydon when they weren't doing armed robberies.

It was a strange building. There were no windows and, other than the fire escape at the back of the kitchen, there was just one way in. The building was detached and was surrounded by a car park. The local myth was that the building had been designed so it would be safe for the Hole in the Wall Gang to plan their robberies. The truth was less interesting. It had originally been a firework warehouse, so had been designed to contain an explosion. That meant thick walls and a thin roof.

And definitely no windows.

Fatty Scraps had turned the warehouse into an Italian restaurant. It was a good business, although its main use was to wash the gang's dirty money. Poe reckoned Fatty Scraps chose the building because it didn't have any windows for nosy police officers to peep through. It was a popular restaurant and did a roaring lunchtime trade. The meatballs in tomato and garlic sauce attracted punters from all over south London.

Poe wasn't keen on Italian food. He preferred the fire and spice of Indian, Korean and Mexican cuisine. He thought Italian food was bland, although he would admit he had never really given it a chance. When he was growing up, Italian food had been freeze-dried pasta mixed with a tin of chopped tomatoes.

He had timed it so the lunchtime crowd was thinning. The waiter was wearing black jeans and a Battista's Bar and Grill polo shirt. Poe followed him to a table.

'Could I have a booth, please?' Poe asked. He pointed at a booth with views of both the kitchen doors and the front entrance. 'That one would be perfect.'

'Of course, sir,' the waiter said.

The seats in the horseshoe-shaped booth were thick and comfortable and covered with red leather. A wipe-clean checked tablecloth, a salt cellar, an enormous pepper grinder and a pot full of grated Parmesan cheese were the only things on the table. Poe assumed the cutlery would be laid out when the waiter knew what he would be eating.

'I will be along with a menu shortly, sir, but in the meantime can I get you a drink?' the waiter asked.

'A pint of whatever you have on draught, please,' Poe said.

While the waiter was at the bar, Poe checked out his surroundings. Other than a couple sharing a bottle of house red, and a hulking brute tucking into a mountain of spaghetti, the restaurant was now empty. Battista's Bar and Grill seemed to be a type of no-frills place for people who wanted nice food at affordable prices. Lots of folk probably paid in cash, ideal for cleaning money. Poe couldn't see Fatty Scraps, but he recognised the man shovelling spaghetti into his mouth as Antony Hanratty, a founding member of the Hole in the Wall Gang.

Hanratty was the gang's safecracker and he went by the nickname Tony Ten-Men. It was a well-deserved nickname. He was the size of a small shed. His hands were like a bunch of bananas and his forearms were thicker than Poe's legs. In his youth he had been a bare-knuckle boxer and he had the flat nose and cauliflower ears to prove it. What he didn't know about old-style safes wasn't worth knowing.

The waiter brought Poe his drink – lager by the looks of it – and a menu. It folded out to three panels, starters on the left, mains in the middle and desserts on the right. Poe didn't bother looking at it.

'I have heard the meatballs are good,' he said.

'Very, sir,' the waiter said.

'Meatballs it is then,' Poe said.

'And what pasta would you like with them, sir?'

That stumped Poe. He had never been to an Italian restaurant on his own before. It had always been for work outings. A leaving do. A Christmas party if he hadn't managed to get his excuses in on time. And if they didn't have a spicy pizza he had someone else order for him. Choosing his own pasta was a new experience.

'What do people usually have with the meatballs?' he said.

'Everyone has their favourite, sir,' the waiter said, 'and it's all prepared fresh.'

'Come on, help me out here. I'm new to this. The only pastas I know are spaghetti and the one that comes in sheets. And those little tube ones that go in macaroni cheese. What are they called?'

'That would be macaroni, sir,' the waiter said, smiling. 'But if you're not sure, I would recommend fettuccine. It's a flat and thick pasta, one of the ribbon types.'

'That works for me,' Poe said, handing back the menu. 'Oh, and can you pass this to the man on that table over there? I think he's called Tony Ten-Men.' He quickly jotted something in his notebook, tore off the page and handed it to the waiter.

'I don't think it's wise to bother him, sir,' the waiter said.

Poe flashed his police ID card. 'Let's do it anyway,' he said.

'Very good, sir,' the waiter said.

'But do me a favour, bring my meatballs first. I get the feeling this is going to be a long afternoon.'

The waiter read the note.

'Maybe not, sir,' he said.

Tony Ten-Men

Things had not gone *exactly* to plan.

The waiter had nervously passed Poe's note to Tony Ten-Men. The ex-bare-knuckle boxer had glanced in Poe's direction, then slipped on a pair of reading glasses. He frowned, looked at Poe again then picked up his phone and spoke briefly. He then went back to his plate of spaghetti. He tore up some bread and dipped it into the rich tomato sauce, ignoring Poe completely.

Any thoughts Poe had that he had been blown off were gone two minutes later when a group of burly men entered the restaurant and stood by the door. Another group came out through the kitchen and blocked that exit. No one had spoken but the message was clear – you are going nowhere.

Tony Ten-Men continued to eat his spaghetti.

The couple sharing the bottle of red wine continued to drink and chat, unaware of the scene playing out in front of them. No one asked them to hurry up. They were allowed to finish in peace.

But eventually they did finish.

The same waiter who had passed the note to Tony Ten-Men helped the couple with their coats and showed them out. The thugs by the door stood to the side, respectful. Poe wondered who the couple were.

The moment they were out the door, Tony Ten-Men got up and walked towards Poe's booth. Without stopping, he said, 'Follow me.'

Poe did.

He followed him all the way into the kitchen.

'Are you showing me your secret sauce?' Poe said.

Tony Ten-Men turned to face Poe. 'Funny,' he said.

He nodded over Poe's shoulder. Before Poe had a chance to turn, a sack was yanked over his head and he was bundled out of the fire exit and thrown into the back of a van. He landed on his elbow. Shooting pains ran up and down his arm and his shoulder began tingling. Someone reached into his pocket and removed his wallet.

'I don't think you realise just how much trouble . . .' Poe started to say.

His protests were cut short by a fist. It jabbed

into his face, filling his mouth with blood. His nose stung and his eyes began to water.

'You don't want me to speak?' Poe asked. 'OK, I'll keep quiet . . . oof!'

It was a boot to the ribs that shut him up this time. Poe thought he heard one of them crack, but that could have been the van door shutting. Another boot to the balls had him doubled up and wheezing.

Had he made a huge mistake?

The sausage factory

Poe was dragged feet first out of the van. His skull cracked against the wet concrete. He ran his tongue across his teeth. One of his fillings had come loose.

Great, he thought.

He was pulled to his feet and pushed into a building. It immediately got colder. He was still wearing a hood and his nose felt like it was full of broken glass, but Poe knew where he was. The smell of raw meat and the sudden drop in temperature meant he was in the meat warehouse the Hole in the Wall Gang had bought twenty years earlier. It was where they cured and air-dried the pork and beef and game meats they served in Battista's Bar and Grill and the other restaurants they owned. It was where the sausages were made.

Poe knew it was also where the gang disposed of anyone who bothered them. The turf wars of the eighties were long over, but all gangs squabbled from time to time. A building whose only purpose was the processing of meat was also perfect for making humans disappear without a trace.

He was marched further inside the warehouse. He heard a metal door open. He was pushed inside a room then thrown to the floor. It was freezing and smelled of meat and blood. The hum of the fridge unit was loud and constant.

'The boss will be here soon,' a voice Poe recognised as Tony Ten-Men said. 'Let's get him up.'

Poe was hauled to his feet. Someone grabbed his arms and his hands were tied together. They were tied at the front, not the back, which Poe thought was odd.

He heard a noise. It was mechanical and clunky, like a conveyor belt with a loose chain. The noise stopped. Something was attached to the rope binding his hands. The noise started again and, without warning, Poe's hands were wrenched up. Pretty soon they were stretched above his head and he was forced to stand on his tiptoes. The noise stopped.

'Higher,' Tony Ten-Men said.

The noise started again and Poe was lifted completely into the air. He could feel himself slowly spinning. He grunted. His arms felt like they were about to tear off.

This was not going well.

'What now?' someone asked.

'We wait,' Tony Ten-Men replied.

'What about him?' the other man asked. 'You want him tuned up a bit?'

'He must be tired. I think he could probably do with a kip, don't you?'

Which was when someone punched Poe in the face and everything went dark.

Meat-hook diplomacy

'Take his hood off,' someone said.

Poe had been drifting in and out of sleep for around ten minutes. He was freezing, groggy, had a splitting headache and the pain from his balls had spread to his stomach. He was still hanging in the air and he was still spinning round.

But he was alive.

A hand grabbed the sack over his head and yanked it off. He squinted in the harsh light, but after a few moments he risked opening his eyes fully. He had been right. He *was* in the gang's meat-packing plant.

He looked up. He was hanging from a meat hook. In his experience, which was limited to bad horror films, anyone hanging from a meat hook was in a dodgy position. Nothing nice happened to people hanging from a meat hook.

He blinked and waited for his eyes to adjust.

The meat-packing plant had two rows of skinned animals. Pigs on one side, cows on the other. Poe was hanging with the pigs. He was close enough to see the slaughterhouse 'Government Inspected' stamps on the animals' haunches and shoulders. He saw the marbled meat and yellow fat, and smelled the iron-rich blood. He was glad Tilly wasn't here. She had been vegan since she was old enough to say, 'I'm not eating that.'

Poe had to wait until he had spun round before he could see who had ordered his hood removed.

Fatty Scraps was sitting on a stool, watching him. Poe knew him from the photographs Tilly had found. Fatty was wearing a thick coat and a woollen hat. When Poe faced him, Fatty stood up and approached him. He was so big he walked like a duck. His face looked soft, like warm ice cream, and he had at least three chins. Tattooed tears dripped from the corners of his hooded eyes. His podgy fingers looked like raw sausages. Despite being in a very cold room, his face was beaded with sweat. Poe thought he was the type of man who would be too hot in an igloo.

The man standing next to Fatty Scraps could not have looked more different. He was as thin as wallpaper and as bald as a snooker ball. He was called Pop 'n' Crisps and he was an original member of the Hole in the Wall Gang. He was Fatty's right-hand man. From what Poe had read, the man's parents had named him Pop 'n' Crisps because that was what he had replied each time they had asked him what he wanted to eat.

'Do you prefer to be called Fatty or Mr Scraps?' Poe asked the big man. He had to raise his voice to be heard above the noise of the fridge unit.

'You are pretty cocky for a man hanging from a meat hook,' Fatty said.

'I have been told I'm more annoying than cocky,' Poe told him.

'That a fact?' Fatty said.

'I'm going to assume you're not a total moron, Mr Scraps,' said Poe. 'And that before you strung me up, you knew *who* you were stringing up.'

Fatty said nothing.

Poe continued, 'You therefore know I'm with the National Crime Agency.'

Pop 'n' Crisps leaned in and whispered into Fatty's ear.

'But you are not here on official business,' Fatty Scraps said, 'which makes this a little confusing.' He thrust Poe's note under his nose. 'Explain this please.'

'It's the address of a jeweller in the West End,' Poe said.

'I can see it's the address of a jeweller in the West End,' said Fatty. 'I want to know why it's written on this piece of paper. What does this address mean to you?'

'I'm thinking of getting my ears pierced,' Poe said.

Fatty nodded towards Tony Ten-Men. The bare-knuckle boxer stepped forward and swung a meaty fist into Poe's stomach. If Poe hadn't been hanging from a meat hook, it would have doubled him over.

'I will ask again,' Fatty said. 'What does this address mean to you?'

Poe took a moment to get his breath back. 'It's a warning,' he gasped. 'One you would be wise to heed.'

A warning

'A warning?' Fatty Scraps said to Poe. 'A warning against what? Is this jeweller swapping their diamonds for cut glass? If so, you have my thanks – Mrs Scraps has been pestering me for a new necklace for a while.'

Poe didn't respond. It was a game of nerves now and he was the one hanging from a meat hook.

'Or maybe it's a warning against something else?' Fatty continued.

Still Poe didn't respond.

'This bleeder is getting right on my nerves, boss,' a shaven-headed thug in a shell suit snarled. 'You want him talking, I'll make him talk.'

The hum of the fridge unit stopped. Poe caught his breath, cocked his head and silently counted to ten. Bang on time, it started again.

Finally, he thought.

'Let me down and I'll talk,' he said.

'You don't come into my place of business and throw demands around, Sergeant Poe,'

Fatty said. 'You talk, I'll listen. If I like what you have to say, I'll cut you down.'

'And if you *don't* like what I have to say?' Poe asked.

'Then I'll just cut you,' Fatty said. 'Maybe turn you into sausages.'

Poe grimaced. He didn't like the sound of that at all.

Fatty grinned. 'Just kidding. I have far too much respect for my customers to serve them minced cop.'

'Well, that's a relief,' Poe said.

'But I *will* take you up to my farm in Epping Forest and feed you to my pigs. They aren't so fussy.'

Poe sighed. Enough of the chest beating – it was time to move things along.

'OK, you get this one for free,' Poe said. 'The address of that jeweller is the next job you have lined up. You plan to go in next Friday afternoon. Pop 'n' Crisps and the guy over there in the purple shell suit, Gavin I think he's called, are on crowd control. They will be wearing clown masks and holding sawn-off shotguns. Tony Ten-Men here will head into the back room with the owner and force him to open the safe. I understand the jeweller will have just taken delivery of some rubies.'

Fatty scowled. 'Is that so?' he said.

Poe nodded. 'And you, Mr Scraps, already have the fence lined up. A Mr Giles Thomasson in Birmingham is expecting them on Sunday morning. He will pay you one hundred and forty-six thousand pounds.'

If it wasn't for the fridge unit, the silence would have been crushing. The Hole in the Wall Gang looked at each other nervously.

'We have a rat,' Fatty said eventually.

'Probably,' Poe said. 'Crews like yours turn on each other eventually. I, on the other hand, prefer more . . . inventive solutions.'

Poe could almost hear the gears turning in Fatty's head.

'Why tell us?' the big man said. 'If you think that's what was going to go down on Friday, why not let us go in then take us on the way out? I know it isn't because you're scared of a West End shoot-out. The National Crime Agency are a bunch of cowboys.'

'I told you,' Poe said. 'This is a warning.'

'I sense a demand coming up,' Fatty said. 'Maybe a payment for future warnings?' He turned to his crew and laughed. 'Honestly, I have yet to meet a cop who isn't as bent as a dog's back leg.'

'This joker has forgotten something though, boss,' Tony Ten-Men said.

'What's that?'

'No one knows he's here. Ten minutes with a blowtorch and we'll know what he knows. If there's a rat, we'll have a name. If there's an operation against us, we'll know that too.'

'What do you say to that, Sergeant Poe?' Fatty asked. 'What's to stop us *taking* the information from you? You see, we can be inventive too.'

'I would say you're just predictable,' Poe said.

Fatty sighed.

'Sergeant Poe, I don't think I'm in the mood to be blackmailed today,' he said. 'Thank you for the warning, but you really should not have come here on your own. It was not a wise decision. So, if you don't mind, I think I'm going to pass. Tony, you know what to . . .'

'You haven't heard what I want yet,' Poe said.

'I know what you want, Sergeant Poe. I know what you *all* want. You want the money. You want the same nice clothes, the fast cars and the big houses we have. God, I bloody hate bent cops.'

'I don't want money, Mr Scraps,' Poe said. He glanced at the man in the shell suit. 'And no offence to that gentleman over there, but I certainly don't want a purple shell suit.'

'I don't care what you want, Sergeant Poe. Because whatever it is, the price will be too high. I didn't get to where I am now by dealing with every bent cop who wants a piece of my action.' He nodded at Tony Ten-Men. 'Take him to the farm.'

'You sure, boss?' said Tony. 'We have never done a cop before.'

'Perhaps it's about time we did then,' said Fatty. 'It will help get the word out we aren't buying any more.'

'Fair enough,' Tony said.

'Any time now would be good,' Poe said.

'What are you in such a hurry for?' Tony Ten-Men said, taking an evil-looking clasp knife from his pocket.

Poe said, 'I wasn't talking to you.'

Which was when Fatty's phone began to ring.

'I would answer that if I were you,' Poe said.

Lemon ice cream

Fatty Scraps looked at Poe craftily. Without a word he removed his phone from his coat pocket.

'Hello?' he said. He listened for a few moments then frowned. 'What text message . . . ?'

He stopped talking. Every member of the Hole in the Wall Gang had just received a text. From Homer Simpson to the Spice Girls, the warehouse rang out with a mish-mash of message alerts.

'I understand there are documents attached to the texts you have just received,' Poe said. 'I advise you to take the time to read them.'

Fatty Scraps put on his reading glasses. Poe allowed himself a wry smile as all but one of the ageing gangsters followed Fatty's example. The one who didn't, the guy in the shell suit, was squinting at his phone like it was an unexpected bill.

Tony Ten-Men was the quickest reader. He slipped his phone in his back pocket and loomed over Poe.

'Who the hell *are* you?' he snapped.

Pop 'n' Crisps glared at his phone, his face white, his mouth hanging open. 'He knows about everything!' he growled. 'My bank accounts, my safety deposit boxes, my houses, everything! He even knows about the money my wife moved abroad last year.'

Fatty didn't respond. No one did. They were all too busy reading their own documents. Poe knew Fatty Scraps had been sent the longest document. Fatty owned more properties, had more bank accounts, more business interests than the others. The man even owned a stable of racehorses. He had more to hide and therefore more to lose.

With no one talking, the hum of the fridge unit seemed even louder. The same way a restaurant's background music seems louder during a lull in the conversation. The unit sort of chugged and gargled and burped with no pattern.

Poe imagined the noise would be like Chinese water torture after a while. It would drive him mad after a week. After six hours in the freezing cold room he would be frozen solid, of course, but it was something to think about while he waited for his fate to be decided.

This had always been the most dangerous part of the plan. Poe thought the Hole in the Wall

Gang would see sense. He thought they would work out that they had little choice other than to do as Poe asked. But there was always a risk someone would act crazy. They might see the red mist, grab one of the nearby meat cleavers and hack his head off before anyone could stop them.

So Poe waited patiently. They had lowered him six inches so at least his feet were on the ground again. His shoulders throbbed, but he didn't think he had suffered any long-term damage.

The Hole in the Wall Gang finished reading their documents one at a time. Only Fatty was left scrolling through the information on his phone. After a minute, he put his iPhone into his jacket pocket.

'OK,' Fatty said. 'You have my attention. What do you want?'

'I wouldn't mind being taken off this meat hook,' Poe replied. 'It's a bit humiliating.'

Fatty Scraps nodded at the thug in the shell suit and a minute later Poe was down and untied. He rubbed some feeling back into his hands. He winced as the pins and needles stung.

'What do you want?' Fatty repeated. 'I assume if we were being taken down, all this would come out in a police interview room, not in a warehouse. This is the start of a negotiation, yes?'

'It is,' Poe answered.

'And you say you don't want money?' Fatty said.

'I don't,' Poe said.

'What *do* you want then?' Fatty asked. 'Property? One of my racehorses? My wife's recipe for lemon ice cream?'

Poe paused. He did like lemon ice cream.

The hum of the fridge unit stopped again. It was a reminder that someone was listening. Someone was watching his back. Telling him to stay focused . . .

'I don't want lemon ice cream,' Poe said, words he never thought he would say, 'and I don't want an animal that craps its pants any time a leaf blows past it.'

'Well, you must want something,' Fatty Scraps said.

'I do,' Poe said.

'What?' Fatty asked.

'I want you to bring Michael Pewter here,' Poe said. 'I want to talk to the Pale Man.'

Fatty Scraps and Pop 'n' Crisps looked at each other.

'Michael?' Fatty Scraps said. 'Why would you want to speak to Michael?'

'And while we wait,' Poe said, ignoring the question, 'I'm going to tell you about a Viking called Harald Bluetooth . . .'

King Harald Bluetooth

'So, to sum up, King Harald Bluetooth united the tribes and formed the Kingdom of Denmark,' Poe said.

'And your point is . . .?' Fatty Scraps said.

'My *point* is that when the company who invented Bluetooth needed a name for technology that unites electronic devices, they thought of the king who united the tribes,' Poe explained. 'The Bluetooth logo is King Harald's joined-up initials in ancient Viking.'

'You would be good on *Who Wants to Be a Millionaire*, Sergeant Poe,' said Fatty.

'Thank you,' said Poe.

'But you're a total gobshite as a prisoner,' Fatty added.

'That's fair enough,' Poe said. 'But if I'm babbling, I'm babbling for a reason. You see, I didn't send you those documents just to force you into bringing Michael Pewter to me.'

'No?' said Fatty.

'No,' said Poe. 'It was also a glimpse into your future.'

'Our future?'

'Actually, it's more accurate to say it's a glimpse into one of your *possible* futures,' Poe said. 'Whether it comes to pass is entirely up to you.'

Fatty looked at his watch. 'Michael is going to be a while,' he said. 'Why don't you look into that crystal ball of yours? Tell us what you see.'

Poe stamped his feet. The floor of the cold-storage warehouse glistened like crushed glass. He rubbed his hands together then put them in his pockets. Any idiot can be cold, he thought.

'The reason I told you about King Harald is because Bluetooth is your weakness,' he said. 'It will *always* be your weakness. Now, the first thing you need to understand is that I work with a remarkable woman. The second thing you need to understand is that this woman doesn't see phones and computers and iPads and smart TVs like you or I do – as things to make our lives better.'

'What does she see them as?' Fatty said.

'She sees them as things to attack,' Poe said. 'She told me that hacking the Bluetooth on your phones was the easiest thing I had ever asked her to do. As we have shown, we have been studying you for a while now and all we had to do was get close to one of you.'

Poe pointed at Pop 'n' Crisps.

'You, to be precise,' Poe continued. 'When you went to the Golden Lion for a rum and Coke last week, we were outside in my car. My friend hacked your Bluetooth and took total control of your phone. And each time you stood near one of your colleagues, we hacked their phone too. It's like a highly contagious electronic disease. A virus. Except this time a vaccine won't be able to help you.'

'You hacked our phones?' Fatty Scraps asked.

'Yes, we did,' Poe said. 'Every part of them. My friend is remotely controlling your microphones as we speak. She is listening and recording every word we say. Do you remember the fridge unit going off?'

Fatty nodded wordlessly. He seemed to be in shock.

'The first time it went off,' Poe said, 'it was her letting me know she was ready to send those documents. The second time was probably her warning me not to get distracted with offers of lemon ice cream.'

Tony Ten-Men moved to turn his phone off.

'I wouldn't do that if I were you,' Poe warned. 'You really don't want to know what happens if she can't hear what is happening in here. She is very . . . protective of me.'

Tony Ten-Men scowled but left his phone switched on.

Poe continued, 'Now, because you all have banking apps and because you thought your emails and texts and social media private messages were secure, I'm afraid it didn't take us long to pull your lives apart. All the stupid codes you used, nothing was secret to us.'

'So why *aren't* we having this conversation at a police station?' Pop 'n' Crisps asked.

'Because I don't care about you,' Poe replied. 'The idiots in the organised crime unit will get you eventually. They don't need my help. They wouldn't thank me if I tried. No, I only want to talk to Michael Pewter.'

Fatty Scraps shook his head. 'Nah, there's something you are not telling me,' he said. 'You could have scooped Michael up with the rest of us. You could have taken us down the nick and talked to him there about whatever you think he has done.'

He removed his phone from his pocket and threw it to Tony Ten-Men.

'Give Terry a bell,' he told him. 'Ask him if he can spare that boy of his for half an hour. Tell him we'll make it worth his while.'

'Will do, boss,' said Tony.

Poe frowned. He didn't know who Terry was. He certainly didn't know who his son was.

Oh well, he thought. As someone once said, no plan survives contact with the enemy.

The Pale Man

Michael Pewter, aka the Pale Man, was the strangest-looking man Poe had ever seen. He was close to seven feet tall and he was completely bald. He didn't even have eyebrows. Barry from the organised crime unit had told Poe that the Pale Man had a condition that caused patches of his skin to lose colour. That might have been the case once, but the condition seemed to have progressed. His head, neck and face were now the colour of milk. It was like he had been washing in bleach. If he had any pink skin left, it was underneath his suit.

And about the suit. It looked like it had been stolen from a 1970s vampire. It was black and long and frayed at the edges. If it had ever been in fashion, it wasn't in the last hundred years.

His eyes were ice-blue and his face was thin. His teeth were perfect and his lips were red. His fingers were long and delicate. Poe thought if he hadn't taken up cutting people, the Pale Man might have been a skilled pianist.

'You wanted to see me, Frank?' he said. His voice was soft and quiet and lisping.

Poe had been thinking of the leader of the Hole in the Wall Gang as Fatty for so long, he had forgotten his parents had named him Frank. Michael Pewter had grown up with Fatty. He had probably called him Frank since they were kids.

'I did, Michael,' Fatty said. 'And I'm sorry I couldn't tell you why. It seems our phones are compromised.'

'It's not a problem. I was in London anyway,' the Pale Man replied. He nodded in Poe's direction. 'We have company, I see. Am I here to deal with him?'

'Maybe,' Fatty said. 'He wants to speak to you first.'

'And who is he?' the Pale Man asked.

'A cop from the National Crime Agency but he's working off-book,' Fatty answered. 'It seems he and his mate have been listening to our conversations. They have been reading our texts and getting into our bank accounts. The West End job is off. They know all about it.'

'And what does he want in return?' asked the Pale Man. 'I assume I wouldn't be here if it was something as crude as an envelope stuffed with twenty-pound notes.'

'He says he doesn't want cash,' Fatty said.

'Or lemon ice cream,' Poe chipped in.

The Pale Man ignored him. 'So . . . ?'

'He says he wants to talk to you,' Fatty Scraps said.

'And then?' the Pale Man asked.

Fatty Scraps shrugged. 'We didn't get that far,' he admitted. 'We have been caught off guard with all this. And be careful what you say. I'm told his friend has remotely accessed the microphones on our phones. She's listening and we can't turn them off.'

The Pale Man turned to Poe. He looked at him with a strange intensity. Poe stared back. The man doesn't blink, he thought. He wondered how many people had spent their last moments on Earth looking into the Pale Man's ice-blue eyes.

The Pale Man produced a beautiful cut-throat razor, the one Poe had been warned about. The one that had sliced throats all over south London. It had a pearl handle and the blade looked sharp enough to cut sunbeams. It was a simple thing. A razor, a handle, which the razor folded into, and a hinge. Three parts, no nonsense. The design hadn't changed in three thousand years. No need for it to change. The craftsmen in ancient Egypt got it right first time.

The razor was easy to keep clean.
It didn't matter what was on the blade.
Shaving foam.
Stubble.
Blood . . .
'So talk,' the Pale Man said.

A Private Matter

'The first thing I want to say, Mr Pewter, is that I'm very sorry about your mum,' Poe said. 'What happened to her was awful. No one deserves . . .'

'Dorothy is dead?' Fatty Scraps interrupted. 'When did this happen, Michael? Why didn't you say anything?'

'It was a private matter,' the Pale Man said. 'I didn't want to bother you.'

'You didn't want to bother . . . Michael, Dorothy was like a mother to me! We grew up in each other's houses! Of course it wouldn't have been a bother. Why on Earth didn't you tell me?'

The Pale Man didn't respond.

'How did she die?' Fatty said. 'Was it her stomach again?'

'If I may?' Poe butted in. 'The *how* is awful, and I won't be saying it out loud. It's the *why* that's important here.'

'The why?' Fatty Scraps said. 'Are you saying she was murdered?'

'As good as. Mr Pewter's mother had been hounded morning, noon and night by a fund-raising foundation. In Mr Pewter's eyes, and on this we are in total agreement, David Gilchrist, the man in charge of the foundation, may as well have killed her himself.'

'Is this true, Michael?' asked Fatty.

The Pale Man kept his eyes on Poe but nodded.

'Who is this Gilchrist geezer?' Fatty Scraps said. 'He's a dead man, he just doesn't know it yet.'

'Oh, I think he does,' Poe said. 'Or he did anyway. David Gilchrist was found tied to a chair in Bristol a week ago. Someone had carved a lump of flesh out of him. No major organs were damaged but whoever did this nicked a major vein and Gilchrist bled out. My unit was called in and it didn't take us long to work out who did it.'

'Answer this with a nod or a shake of the head, Michael,' Fatty Scraps said, aware that Tilly could hear every word being said. 'Did you kill this man?'

The Pale Man didn't hesitate. He nodded immediately. He had probably never lied to Fatty Scraps in his life.

Fatty turned to Poe. 'This is all a bit elaborate, isn't it?' He gestured towards the meat hook.

'Couldn't you have just arrested Michael at his home? Why put yourself through all this?'

'Mr Pewter knows what he's doing,' Poe said. 'He didn't leave a scrap of evidence behind and, other than a strong motive, we have nothing that links him to the murder of David Gilchrist. And if we tested that razor he's holding, I doubt we would find a scrap of DNA on it.'

'So if you're not here to arrest him, and you're not here for a bung,' Fatty said, 'what *are* you here for?'

'I'm here to persuade Mr Pewter to hand himself in,' Poe said. 'I would like him to walk into Broadbury Road Police Station in Bristol, ask for Detective Chief Inspector Lucy Sampson and make a full confession. He will be charged with manslaughter rather than murder, and the file into why his mother died will be made available to his defence team. Usually the sentence would be at least fifteen years in prison, but a defence that he lost control of himself will be accepted. If Mr Pewter pleads guilty he will be sentenced to six years in prison.'

'Really?' asked Fatty.

'Yes, really,' Poe said.

'Six years for killing the bastard who did in his dear old mum?' Fatty said. 'Six years when he should be getting a medal?'

'The law doesn't work like that,' Poe said.

Fatty Scraps frowned. 'You have just said you have nothing on him,' he said. 'Why would Michael hand himself in?'

'That's where you come in,' Poe said.

Jon

'Are you bleeding mental?' Fatty yelled. 'I have known Michael since we were grubby little five-year-olds playing in the gutter. Why the hell would I ask him to turn himself in?'

Poe said nothing.

'What, you think just because you have hacked into our bank accounts and know what jobs we have lined up, we are just going to roll over and turn on our own?' Fatty continued. 'It isn't happening, my friend! We can get new phones. We can disable Bluetooth. We can change how we communicate. This is a setback, but that's all it is. It certainly isn't the total disaster you seem to think . . .'

Fatty paused. The door to the meat room had opened. Terry's son, the man Tony Ten-Men had called for, had arrived.

'Right, let's see how much trouble we are really in,' Fatty continued.

It seemed Terry's son was a lawyer. He was called Jon and he was there to advise the Hole in the Wall Gang. Fatty quickly explained what was happening. When he had finished, Jon said, 'And Sergeant Poe definitely doesn't have a warrant?'

'He doesn't,' Fatty said. 'We have checked. He seems to be working off-book.'

'And he hasn't asked for a bribe?' Jon asked.

'No. He just wanted to speak to Michael,' Fatty told him. 'He wants him to own up to a murder.'

'And will he?' Jon said.

'He isn't keen,' Fatty replied.

'And nor should he be,' Jon said. 'By the sounds of it, Sergeant Poe's friend has used illegal methods to hack your phones. And even if she hasn't, if the police don't have a warrant you have nothing to worry about.'

'You sure?' Fatty asked.

'Positive,' Jon said. 'It's a clear violation of your right to a private life. Sergeant Poe has broken the law. *He* has more chance of seeing the inside of a prison cell than any of you do.'

'Thank you, Jon,' Fatty said. 'You should probably leave now.'

Jon said. 'Dad has asked me to pass on his good wishes to your old lady.'

'Tell him we'll have a meal at Battista's next week,' Fatty said.

'I'll do that,' Jon said. 'Stay lucky.'

And without looking back, Jon left the warehouse.

'Turn off your phones, boys,' Fatty Scraps said. 'This fool has threatened us in our own house. It is time to let Michael do what he does best.'

The Pale Man stepped forward, the cut-throat razor glinting wickedly in his hand. He held it low but Poe knew it would soon be at his throat. Tony Ten-Men and Pop 'n' Crisps held Poe steady.

'Any last words?' Fatty Scraps said.

Poe burst out laughing.

'You lot are even stupider than I thought,' he said.

The rules of the game

'What's so funny?' Fatty Scraps snapped. 'From where I am, you're the fool about to get a wet neck.'

'You don't seriously think I came in here to threaten you with the law, did you?' said Poe.

Fatty scowled but he held up his hand to stop the Pale Man. 'Let him speak, Michael,' he said.

'I know what we did was illegal,' Poe said. 'Of course it was. You can't just go around remotely controlling people's phones. No court in the land is going to give the police permission to do that, not without specific intelligence. Which of course we didn't have.'

'I'm not sure how this helps, Sergeant Poe,' Fatty said. 'All you are doing is confirming what Jon told us.'

'Yes,' Poe said, 'but that's because Jon thinks I play by my rules. The police rules.'

'And let me guess, you don't?' said Fatty.

'No,' Poe said. 'I play by *your* rules.'

'What the hell does that mean?' asked Fatty.

'It means if I don't leave here intact, or if I do but Mr Pewter refuses to cooperate,' Poe said, 'my friend goes to work.'

'But you already said, we can't be touched by the police,' Fatty said. 'There is nothing she can do to us.'

'You sure about that?' Poe asked.

'I am,' said Fatty. 'You might have a pair of kings, but we're holding four aces. And now I'm tired of listening to your stupid northern accent.'

Fatty Scraps nodded at the Pale Man. Poe ignored the advancing killer.

'Here's what happens if that razor touches my neck,' Poe said. 'My colleague will unleash the kind of hell never seen before in London. Total carnage.'

'Oh yeah? And how's she going to do that?' Fatty asked.

'The first thing she will do is tell the police about the smuggling ring the East End Albanians are running,' Poe said.

'What smuggling ring?' Fatty said. 'And what the hell's that got to do with us?'

'Everything, as it happens,' Poe replied. 'You see, we didn't just read your texts and your emails and your sad WhatsApp messages. We also used your bank accounts to register you all as undercover sources.' He grinned. 'Congratulations, gentlemen, each one of you is now an official Metropolitan Police informant. Grasses, I think you might call them down here. Or is it snitches?'

'You did what?!' Fatty Scraps screamed.

Fatty's face had gone from smug to panic in less than a second. Poe thought that had to be some kind of record. He eyed the rest of the Hole in the Wall Gang. Their faces were white with fear. The police might not scare them, but being known as a grass certainly did. In their world, snitches got a lot more than stitches. They were likely to be stuffed behind a dumpster with a dead rat in their mouth.

'And after one of you has had the money put into their bank account for grassing up the Albanians, my friend will start hacking the phones of the Turkish-Cypriots, the Russians and the Ukrainians,' Poe continued. 'And each time my friend uncovers something, she will pass it to the Met under one of your names. How long before some dirty cop realises he has something valuable to other criminals? How long before your names are for sale? A month? Two? Certainly no more than three. What happens then?'

None of them had an answer.

'Let's face it, I am now the war you cannot win,' Poe said. 'Now, I'm told you are old school. You don't hurt women or kids. I wish I could say the same about the new breed of gangster. Those gangsters won't just kill you. They will hurt your families.'

'And if Michael confesses?' Fatty asked.

'Then you get to keep your reputation,' Poe said. 'And your kneecaps aren't removed with a blowtorch.'

'That's it?' Fatty said. 'If Michael does his time, it's over?'

'As far as I'm concerned. You will still be on the organised crime unit's radar, but you won't be on mine.'

Fatty Scraps faced the Pale Man.

'Michael? I can't force you to do this,' he said. 'But you know as well as I do what happens if we get labelled as grasses. It's not just us, it's our families, our friends, everyone will get hurt.' He paused. 'But, say the word and we will see if there's another way.'

'I will do the time, Frank,' the Pale Man said. 'Six years is nothing.'

'Are you sure?' Fatty asked.

The Pale Man said, 'It will give me time to remember my mum.'

The two men hugged and Poe was reminded

how close they were. Among a certain type of criminal there was still honour. Fatty turned back to Poe.

'It seems we have a deal,' Fatty said. 'Is there anything else I can help you with, Sergeant Poe?'

'Actually, now you come to mention it, there is something,' Poe said. 'And it is non-negotiable, I'm afraid.'

Conference Room 18

Conference Room 18, National Crime Agency Headquarters, Citadel Place, London.

'OK, thank you,' Poe said. He put his phone back into his jacket pocket and gently knocked on the door of the conference room. He slipped in quietly. He caught someone's eye on the five-person panel. The man raised his eyebrows and Poe nodded once. Poe then retook his seat in between Tilly and his boss, Detective Inspector Stephanie Flynn. The room was hot and stuffy. Poe was soon sweating under his collar again. The disciplinary meeting had been going for an hour now, and there was no sign it would be over soon.

Justin Hanson was the director of the organised crime unit. He was the fool that Flynn had been arguing with a week or so ago when Tilly had been explaining what would happen if the world's population arrived in Cumbria and jumped up and down. Hanson liked the sound of his own voice too much. He used to be the deputy director of intelligence, the department that oversaw Poe's unit, but had been promoted to head up the organised crime unit. He and Poe had always hated each other.

Hanson was talking when Poe had left the room to answer his phone and he was still talking now. He was questioning Barry, one of the organised crime sergeants Poe had met in Bristol. Barry was even angrier than Hanson that Poe had been poking around in his database and carrying out illegal acts against the Hole in the Wall Gang.

'By being reckless, he has ruined five years of careful undercover work,' Barry said.

Hanson sneered. Poe saw him write down 'reckless' and underline it three times.

Poe's own director, Director of Intelligence Edward van Zyl, was there too, but he had not said anything. As Poe's director, Van Zyl wouldn't get a vote on whether Poe was guilty. Only the three members of the panel who weren't involved in the case would vote. It was a pity, as Van Zyl had always helped Poe. The upside was that Hanson wouldn't get a vote either, because he had filed the charges against Poe.

'And can you confirm that Sergeant Poe was told to stay away from Michael Pewter?' Hanson asked, adding to his attack on Poe.

'I could not have been clearer, sir,' Barry replied.

'And did you give him permission to look at the information we have collected on the Hole in the Wall Gang?' Hanson asked.

'Absolutely not,' Barry said.

Barry turned to Poe and glared. Poe stuck his tongue out. Sometimes it was fun to be childish.

'Point of order,' Edward van Zyl said. It was the first time he had spoken. 'I don't believe Sergeant Poe *did* contact Michael Pewter, the so-called Pale Man. As I understand it, Pewter came to him.'

'While I was hanging from a meat hook,' Poe chipped in, earning himself another glare from Barry and Hanson.

'It was obvious that Poe was not meant to contact *any* of the Hole in the Wall Gang, Edward!' Hanson snapped. 'He was told to stay away and he didn't. It's as simple as that. And he then threatened them with being labelled informants. That is beyond the pale!'

'Hey, I wasn't actually going to do it,' Poe said, grinning.

Hanson ignored him. 'Now, can we move on to the damage Sergeant Poe's *reckless* actions have caused,' he said.

Poe sighed. He leaned in and whispered in

Flynn's ear, 'Did Hanson say anything sensible while I was outside?'

'Not really,' she said. 'Who was that on the phone?'

'I will tell you later.' He leaned across the other way. 'How are you holding up, Tilly?'

Disciplinary meetings were routine to Poe, but this was Tilly's first.

'I'm OK, Poe,' she said. 'Are your testicles still aching?'

Flynn sniggered. Poe winced at the memory of being kicked.

'Director Justin Hanson has been saying some awfully mean things about you, Poe,' Tilly continued.

'Yeah, he's a dickhead,' Poe said. 'Has he mentioned that I don't have the skills to do what he's accusing me of? That I could no more breach a secure database than I could lick my own elbow?'

'He hasn't, Poe,' Tilly said.

'And he's not mentioned you?' Poe asked.

'Not once,' Tilly replied.

'He's not that stupid then.'

Poe wasn't surprised Hanson had decided to leave Tilly out of this. Nobody wanted to mess with someone who could do the things she could. Annoy her and you would never be able to trust anything electronic ever again. Tilly had watched Poe eat eight sausages for his tea one night. For the next month, every time he got in his car his satnav directed him to a vegan supermarket in Belgium.

He had to eat an apple before she would change it back.

A kick in the nuts

Thirty minutes later, Hanson finally ran out of steam. He finished moaning and handed the floor to Director of Intelligence Edward van Zyl.

'Sergeant Poe,' Van Zyl said, 'you left the room a while back to take a phone call. Can you tell us who it was from?'

'Yes, sir,' Poe answered. 'It was Detective Chief Inspector Lucy Sampson from Avon and Somerset Police. She's the detective who called us after the murder in Bristol.'

'Did she have anything interesting to say?' asked Van Zyl.

'She did,' Poe said. 'An hour ago, Michael Pewter, the hired killer sometimes called the Pale Man, walked into Broadbury Road Police Station and confessed to the murder of David Gilchrist. He states that he did not mean to kill him, but it was by his cut-throat razor that Gilchrist died. He described how and when he did it, the weapon he used and why. Mr Pewter states his actions were his own and his own only. As expected, he was taking revenge against the man he says is to blame for the death of his mother.'

'I take it Detective Chief Inspector Sampson is happy?' Van Zyl asked.

'Very, sir,' Poe said.

'A good result then?' Van Zyl said.

'Yes, sir.'

'This is irrelevant!' Hanson snapped. 'The fact that this man has confessed does not matter. This panel has been convened to investigate the fact that Sergeant Poe clearly broke the rules. I think we are done here, so unless you have anything else to add, Edward, I suggest we move to a vote right now.'

'There is one more thing, as it happens,' Van Zyl said.

'Oh yeah?' Hanson sneered. 'What is it this time? Sergeant Poe doesn't have to obey the rules the rest of us live by because he gets results? I warned you Poe would be your downfall one day, Edward. I believe that day has now come.'

'Your constant warnings did you credit, Justin,' Van Zyl smiled, 'but on this occasion, I'm afraid they were not needed.'

'And why not?' Hanson asked.

'Because Sergeant Poe didn't break any rules,' Van Zyl said.

'What? Of course he did, man! He's already admitted using the organised crime unit's own intelligence in his silly operation. That's all the proof this panel needs. Now, can we please vote . . .'

'He has not broken any rules, Justin, because at all times Sergeant Poe was working under my direction. *I* gave him access to the organised crime unit's intelligence. Sergeant Poe did not hack your database. He had permission to look at it.'

'Nonsense!' Hanson snarled. 'Permission can only be given by me. And I think I would remember if Sergeant Poe's name had crossed my desk.'

'I'm sure you would.' Van Zyl reached into his inside pocket and took out a document. He passed it to Hanson. 'But as you will see, permission came from your boss, the director-general herself.'

'B-b-but why would she go over my head?' Hanson stammered.

'I think this is best explained by Sergeant Poe,' Van Zyl said.

Poe stood.

'Thank you, sir,' he said. 'Apart from being kicked in the nuts and being hung from a meat hook, there was one other thing that caught my attention during this operation . . .'

A dog's back leg

'I have yet to meet a cop who isn't as bent as a dog's back leg,' Poe said to the panel. 'That's what Fatty Scraps said to me.'

'Are you suggesting that in the past he has paid police officers for information, Sergeant Poe?' the chair of the panel, and its only female member, asked.

'Yes,' Poe said. 'But that's not all.'

'No?'

'No,' Poe said. 'You see, one of the first things Pop 'n' Crisps said to Fatty Scraps was that I wasn't there on official business. And a few minutes later, Tony Ten-Men said,' – Poe checked his notes to make sure he got it right – '"This joker has forgotten something though, boss. No one knows he's here." Somehow, the gang knew that I could not have been there on official business.'

'And what did you take from that, Sergeant Poe?' Van Zyl asked.

'This told me that not only had Fatty Scraps

paid for information in the past, sir, but he still had a source of information inside the National Crime Agency. He still had someone he could call in real time if there was a problem.'

'You thought we had an informant, a mole?' asked Van Zyl.

'I did, sir. It was the only thing that made sense. No one outside the National Crime Agency could have confirmed I was conducting an unofficial operation.'

'Even though, in fact, you *had* been authorised,' Van Zyl said. 'Not only had you been given permission to examine the organised crime unit's intelligence, you also had a warrant allowing you to electronically eavesdrop on the Hole in the Wall Gang.'

'Yes, sir. But that information wasn't widely available at the time. If someone had checked our database to see what cases I was working on, the Hole in the Wall Gang would not have shown up.'

'And that is because, apart from you, Miss Tilly Bradshaw and DI Flynn, only myself and the director-general knew what was happening?' asked Van Zyl.

'Yes, sir,' Poe replied.

'So, even though you were working on an official case, the information the gang received from their mole would have been that you weren't,' Van Zyl said.

'That's right, sir,' Poe said.

'This is outrageous!' Hanson protested. 'This entire operation has been conducted in secret! The second we leave this room I will be banging on the director-general's door, demanding an explanation. She cannot undermine me like this!'

'That is your right, Justin,' Van Zyl said calmly. 'What did you do next, Sergeant Poe?'

'I got beaten up a bit, sir,' Poe said. 'But after I explained what the gang's choices were, we managed to have a sensible discussion.'

'And now Michael Pewter has made a full confession?' Van Zyl asked.

'Yes, sir,' Poe said.

'And that, as I remember, was your one and only goal,' Van Zyl said.

'Yes, sir,' Poe said. 'I had no interest in the Hole in the Wall Gang.'

'How about a bent copper?' Van Zyl asked.

'That's a different matter, sir,' Poe said. 'On this Fatty Scraps and I agree – we both hate bent cops. For him, they are the cost of doing business. For me, they are the pea under my mattress, the pebble in my shoe. If I know a bent copper is out there and it's a choice between dealing with it myself or leaving it to someone else, well, sir, that's no choice at all.'

'So what did you do about it?' Van Zyl asked.

'I need help explaining this, sir.' Poe turned to Tilly and said, 'Over to you, Tilly.'

The mole

Tilly spent a moment linking her laptop to the screen on the wall. It was not lost on Poe that she did this via Bluetooth. She faced the panel. If she was nervous, she didn't show it. Poe wasn't surprised. To people who did not know her, Tilly could appear gentle. Timid, even. But Poe *did* know her. And beneath her bookish exterior beat the heart of a lion.

Simply put, she was the bravest person he had ever met. She had faced down serial killers. She had rescued him from a burning building. She had been in the middle of a bar fight. And she had listened to him being beaten by Tony Ten-Men and still held firm. A panel of senior officers was not about to scare her.

'My name is Tilly Bradshaw,' she said, 'and I was listening while Poe was in the restaurant and, later, when he was in the meat warehouse.'

'You were his only helper?' a male panel member asked. 'Just you?'

'Yes, sir. Poe said I was more than enough.'

'Really?' he said.

'I'm here, aren't I?' Poe said.

'I suppose you are,' the panel member said. 'Please continue, Miss Bradshaw.'

'At first I was only listening through Poe's phone, but the moment he was taken from the restaurant I believed the need had been met.'

'The need for what?' asked the man.

'The need to go beyond what was in the warrant,' she replied. 'The need to remotely access the microphones on the Hole in the Wall Gang's phones and listen to what was happening in the warehouse.'

Poe nodded to himself. He and Tilly had practised that bit. What they had done was technically illegal. Permission to control the Hole in the Wall Gang's phone microphones was not on the warrant, but if Poe's life was put at risk, a different set of rules applied. If that happened, Tilly was allowed to do anything she thought necessary. The moment he was bundled into a warehouse and hung from a meat hook, she had all the excuses she needed. The fact Poe had *planned* on his life being put at risk was neither here nor there.

Tilly brought up an audio file. She dragged her fingers across her laptop's track pad and positioned the arrow. She clicked play and the Pale Man's voice filled the room.

'I will do the time, Frank,' the Pale man said. 'Six years is nothing.'

Tilly pressed pause. 'That was Michael Pewter speaking to Frank Mason, known as Fatty Scraps,' she said. 'He was agreeing to confess to the murder of David Gilchrist.'

She pressed play again.

'Are you sure?' Fatty Scraps said.

'It will give me time to remember my mum,' the Pale Man said.

'It seems we have a deal,' Fatty Scraps said.

Tilly pressed pause.

She said, 'And that was Fatty Scraps agreeing to Poe's demands.'

She pressed play.

'Good,' Poe said on the recording.

'Is there anything else I can help you with, Sergeant Poe?' Fatty Scraps asked.

'Actually, now you come to mention it, there is something,' Poe said. 'And it is non-negotiable, I'm afraid.'

Tilly paused again. She looked at Van Zyl. He nodded for her to continue. For the first time she looked nervous. Poe knew why. He knew what was about to happen.

She hit play again.

'I want the name of the mole inside the National Crime Agency's organised crime unit,' Poe said to Fatty Scraps.

An unbroken silence followed. The panel members looked at each other uneasily.

'Is there a problem with the recording, Miss Bradshaw?' one of them asked.

'As if I have problems with things like this,' she snorted.

Poe winced. It did not matter who Tilly was speaking to, if someone doubted her computer skills they got a snarky comment in return.

'No,' Tilly continued, 'this was the time Frank Mason took to consider Poe's request.'

After five minutes of silence, Fatty Scraps spoke again.

'And if I don't?' he said.

Poe said, 'Then my colleague will use one of your names to snitch on the Russians about the brothel they are running in Covent Garden. She has the information all ready to go.'

'I need another minute,' Fatty said.

'Take all the time you need,' Poe said. 'It's a big decision.'

It was closer to two minutes than one before Fatty Scraps started talking again.

'OK, let's say we do have someone on the inside,' he said. 'And let's say I'm willing to give you his or her name. How can I possibly do it without dropping myself in it? A cop taking a bung will get in trouble, but so will the man paying him.'

Tilly pressed pause. Poe stood up.

'At this point I was improvising,' Poe said to the members of the panel. 'I hadn't known about the mole but, as soon as I did, finding out who he or she was became my number one priority. So I did what I thought was best at the time.'

Tilly pressed play again. Poe's voice came through the speakers once more.

'I can offer you immunity,' he said. 'If one of you wants to turn on their voice recorder app, I will confirm this for your records.'

'You aren't allowed to offer immunity!' Hanson yelled. 'How dare you take decisions like that!'

Tilly paused the recording.

'You're quite correct, sir, I *don't* have the right,' Poe said. 'But I looked at the bigger picture and decided that giving Fatty Scraps a pass on bribing a cop was outweighed by the need to find out who the bent cop was.'

'Nevertheless!' Hanson snapped. 'I want this panel disbanded until we have got to the bottom of what has happened here.'

'What, before the vote, Justin?' Van Zyl smiled.

'I believe,' Hanson continued, 'that by offering immunity to a known criminal, Sergeant Poe has broken the law. Sergeant Poe should not be allowed to give any further evidence. It's for his own good.'

'I'm OK, thanks,' Poe said.

'This isn't up to you, Poe!' Hanson shouted.

'No, but it is up to me, Justin,' the female chair of the panel said. 'And I would like to hear what Sergeant Poe has to say. We can decide what actions to take afterwards. Sergeant Poe, please continue.'

'Thank you,' Poe said. 'Anyway, I figured I wasn't doing too much damage giving these clowns a pass. It was a small price to pay. They are so dumb that we would have no problem bringing them down later if they no longer had their mole protecting them. I also figured if the mole was getting money from the Hole in the Wall Gang, he was probably getting money from other criminal gangs as well.'

The panel chair nodded in agreement.

Poe said, 'Press play please, Tilly.'

Tilly did. Fatty Scraps began talking.

'OK,' he said. 'I'll give you the name of this arsehole, but first I do want you making a statement on the record that we have immunity. Tony, can you do the honours?'

The next five minutes were filled with Poe making a verbal statement about the Hole in the Wall Gang's immunity. When Tony had checked that the voice recording had worked, Fatty Scraps said, 'To be honest, I'll be glad to get rid of this greedy bastard. He was never happy with what we were giving him. He was always wanting more, always moaning about the risks he was taking. I told him, he should try going to work with a shotgun and a sledge-hammer.'

'I told you they were not that bright,' Poe said to the panel as the recording continued. 'He said this even though he knew Tilly was listening.'

On Tilly's recording, Fatty Scraps asked, 'How do you want to do this?'

'I want the name of your insider and I want details of how he was paid,' Poe said. 'I want to know how much money he got and what information you received in return. If I find out later on that you have missed off anything, the immunity agreement is void. I will come after you with everything.'

'OK, OK, keep your hair on,' said Fatty Scraps.

'The name?' Poe said.

In the conference room, Hanson stood up and Tilly paused the recording.

'I'm not feeling very well,' Hanson said.

'I think we may have to stop the meeting. I need to go and lie down.'

'Sit down!' Van Zyl hissed.

Hanson had lost so much colour he was almost see-through. He remained standing though, a spark of defiance burning in his beady eyes.

Van Zyl said, 'I swear if you don't sit down, Justin, I will have uniformed officers come in and pin you to your seat!'

Hanson stared at Van Zyl and saw that he was not kidding. He sat.

Tilly pressed play.

'It's someone you know, actually,' Fatty Scraps said.

'Someone I know?' Poe said.

'Well, he knows you,' Fatty Scraps said. 'He doesn't seem to like you either.'

'That doesn't really narrow things down,' Poe said. 'Lots of people don't like me. Who is the mole?'

'It's the director of the organised crime unit himself,' Fatty Scraps said. 'It's Justin Hanson.'

Caught red-handed

'This is shameful!' Hanson cried, lurching to his feet. His chair tipped over but he made no move to pick it up. 'What a farce! We surely are *not* taking the word of a cockney villain over a highly decorated police officer! I'll sue Fatty Scraps for everything he's got!'

He glared at Van Zyl.

'And don't you dare tell me to sit down again, Edward!' Hanson continued. 'Playing this recording in front of the lesser ranks is totally unacceptable! And how do we know Poe hasn't fiddled with this recording? It is not a secret that we don't see eye to eye.'

'I wouldn't know how to fiddle with it,' Poe said, smiling.

'She would, though!' Hanson shouted, pointing at Tilly. 'And she does what Poe says. No court would convict me on this, let alone a British one.'

'You're quite right, Justin,' Van Zyl replied calmly. 'This recording is not enough to convict you.'

'Finally, a bit of common sense,' Hanson said. 'Not before time either. This is all madness!'

'But it *was* enough for the director-general to sign off on another warrant,' Van Zyl said. 'For the last two weeks Miss Bradshaw has been going through your bank accounts, your travel movements and your phone records. In short, she's turned your life upside down.'

'Oh God,' Hanson said.

'Indeed,' Van Zyl said. 'It seems you have amassed quite the fortune, Justin. And not just from the Hole in the Wall Gang. Miss Bradshaw found payments going back nine years from fifteen different gangs. We also opened the safety deposit box you think no one knows about, and we have the gold and jewellery you had tucked away. In total, you have over two million pounds in cash and assets. Now, I'm not a legal expert, but I would say we have more than enough. Wouldn't you?'

Hanson said nothing. He slumped in his seat, put his head in his hands and started to sob. A string of snot left one nostril, a bubble popped in the other.

'At least you have kept your dignity, sir,' Poe said.

'That's enough, Sergeant Poe,' Van Zyl said. He stood. 'Justin Hanson, I am arresting you for corruption as detailed in Section 26 of the Criminal Justice and Courts Act 2015.'

* * *

With Hanson in handcuffs and on his way to a police cell, the chair of the panel said, 'I have to say, Edward, that was one of the more entertaining disciplinary panels I have chaired. And, Sergeant Poe?'

'Yes?' Poe answered.

'Well done,' she said.

'Thank you.'

And with that the meeting ended.

'I think you deserve a drink, Sergeant Poe,' Van Zyl said.

Poe nodded, then turned to Tilly and Flynn. 'Can I meet you guys in the pub over the road?' he asked. 'I just want a quick word with the director.'

When they had left the room, Poe looked Van Zyl in the eyes and said, 'You bastard.'

Bait

'Do you know what has bothered me about this case from the very beginning?' Poe asked.

'I don't think I do, Sergeant Poe,' Van Zyl replied, his eyes twinkling.

'It was something Detective Chief Inspector Sampson told me. She said her chief constable had told her to bring in our unit to help her.'

'And why would this bother you?' Van Zyl asked. 'Surely your unit's role is to help local police forces when they get murders like the one she was investigating?'

'It is, but we are normally called in with reluctance. The local cops usually want to try to crack the case first, but the body was still warm when Detective Chief Inspector Sampson called Detective Inspector Flynn. In my experience, that *never* happens.'

'What can I tell you, Poe?' Van Zyl said. 'Perhaps she's the exception that proves the rule?'

'Rubbish,' Poe snapped. 'You *knew* there was

a mole in the organised crime unit. It's the only thing that makes sense.'

Van Zyl remained silent for several moments. He seemed to be weighing up what he could and couldn't say. 'I didn't know,' he said eventually. 'But the director-general did.'

'The director-general?' Poe said, amazed.

'She has her fingers in all the pies and she knew something was a bit off,' Van Zyl explained. 'The organised crime unit has had some big failures recently, far more than could be put down to bad luck. So yes, the director-general suspected they had a bad apple. She approached me and asked me if I had any ideas.'

'And you did?' asked Poe.

Van Zyl nodded. 'As it happened, one of our fraud units had been investigating David Gilchrist's foundation and, when Dorothy Pewter stepped in front of that train, I saw our chance. Her son Michael, the Pale Man, was involved with one of the gangs that were *too* lucky.

'We suspected the gang of having some inside help from the police. I thought there was an outside chance the Pale Man might find out his mother had been terrorised by this foundation and would take his revenge. So yes, I asked Avon and Somerset's chief constable to call in your unit immediately if anything happened to David Gilchrist.'

'You used David Gilchrist as bait?' Poe asked.

Van Zyl shrugged. 'A hired killer's mum threw herself in front of a train because of Gilchrist. There was always going to be a price to pay.'

'We could have protected Gilchrist,' Poe said.

'How? And for how long?' asked Van Zyl. 'You have read the reports on the Pale Man. He would have got to Gilchrist eventually. So I got the director-general on board. I said that if David Gilchrist was murdered, you should be given everything you asked for to help you chase down his killer. That's why the director-general signed off on the warrant and the electronic surveillance.

'We had no idea what would happen, but when you are involved in cases things have a habit of getting bigger than they start out. And we felt if you were allowed to follow the evidence wherever it took you, there was half a chance you and Tilly would go up against the Pale Man's employer, the Hole in the Wall Gang.'

Poe said nothing.

'And really, has anything bad happened?' Van Zyl continued. 'A corrupt police officer is behind bars and a killer has made a confession. I will sleep fine tonight.'

'They hung me from a bloody meat hook,' Poe said. 'They kicked me in the balls and told me I would be fed to their pigs. I would call that pretty bad.'

'But Miss Bradshaw was watching over you,' Van Zyl said. 'You were perfectly safe.'

'That's not the point!' Poe said.

'Well, what is the point, Sergeant Poe?' Van Zyl asked.

'You could have told me what the end game was.'

'And told you we had a mole in organised crime?' Van Zyl said. 'Do you think the director-general should share information like that with a sergeant?'

Poe folded his arms and scowled. 'I don't like being used,' he said. 'And I don't like Tilly being used.'

'But surely it's your job to be used,' Van Zyl said. 'I use you, Detective Chief Inspector Sampson used you, and the *public* uses you. We all use you, Sergeant Poe. And that's not a bad thing. We sleep safer *because* we use you.'

Poe sighed. How did you win against an argument like that? 'Grab your coat, sir,' he said.

'Are we going somewhere?' Van Zyl asked.

'We are going to the pub,' Poe said.

'We are?'

'And you are going to explain all this to Tilly and the boss,' Poe said.

For a moment Poe thought Van Zyl might refuse. 'Fine,' Van Zyl said. 'And I enjoy the occasional pale ale, as it happens. I will have just the one drink, though.'

'Oh no, sir,' Poe said. 'We will be out all night and the only person who will be opening his wallet is you. You are going to pay for us to get drunk and then we are going for something to eat.'

'I'm paying for your food as well?' Van Zyl asked.

'What do you think?' Poe replied.

'And where are we going?'

'I don't care,' Poe said. 'As long as it's not Battista's Bar and Grill . . .'

About Quick Reads

"Reading is such an important building block for success"

- Jojo Moyes

Quick Reads are short books written by best-selling authors. They are perfect for regular readers and those who are still to discover the pleasure of reading.

Did you enjoy this Quick Read?

Tell us what you thought by filling in our short survey. Scan the QR code to go directly to the survey or visit https://bit.ly/QuickReads2022 or scan the QR code

Turn over to find your next Quick Read...

A special thank you to Jojo Moyes for her generous donation and support of Quick Reads and to **Here Design**.

Quick Reads is part of The Reading Agency, a national charity tackling life's big challenges through the proven power of reading.

www.readingagency.org.uk
@readingagency #QuickReads

The Reading Agency Ltd. Registered number: 3904882 (England & Wales)
Registered charity number: 1085443 (England & Wales)
Registered Office: 24 Bedford Row, London, WC1R 4EH
The Reading Agency is supported using public funding by Arts Council England.

Find your next Quick Read: the 2022 series

Available to buy in paperback or ebook and to borrow from your local library.

More from Quick Reads

For a complete list of titles and more information on the authors and their books visit

www.readingagency.org.uk/quickreads

THE READING AGENCY

Continue your reading journey

The Reading Agency is here to help keep you and your family reading:

Challenge yourself to complete six reads by taking part in **Reading Ahead** at your local library, college or workplace
readingahead.org.uk

Join **Reading Groups for Everyone** to find a reading group and discover new books
readinggroups.org.uk

Celebrate reading on **World Book Night** every year on 23 April
worldbooknight.org

Read with your family as part of the **Summer Reading Challenge** at your local library
summerreadingchallenge.org.uk

READING GROUPS FOR EVERYONE

SUMMER READING CHALLENGE

For more information, please visit our website:
readingagency.org.uk